Blackstrap's Ecstasy

Blackstrap's Ecstasy:

A Corsair Captain's Log

J. J. M. Czep

Clayborn
press

Special thanks to:

Shaun, for putting up with poor house keeping, strange sleep schedules, and bizarre discussions and debates about things that never happened that come from being wed to a writer.

Stacy, for all of her assistance, love and amazing editing skills!

Danielle, for making fun of my horrible Asian language usage and fixing some of the more vile mistakes.

Margaret, for editing and inspiring!

Max, without whom Blackstrap, and a very important piece of my soul would not exist.

And to my mom and dad, of course, for not committing their strange daughter for an over active imagination

Chapter 1

...and if you asked...

...I didn't ask...

The mountain of patchwork quilt waved, a sun-weathered hand gripped the pale linen of the feather pillow. Gennie shifted in restless sleep. The composed voice in her dream tugged at memories, dabbled at making nightmares of happier times, and chanted its demand a maddening mantra, "ask...ask...ask...". Sleeping eyelids constricted, knuckles whitened, Gennie gripped and pulled the wadded sheets. A noise that awake might have been a scream escaped her parted lips as a strangled yelp. Gennie's body shot upright, escaping the voice at last. Her abrupt arousal scattered the young man sharing the captain's bed and quarters from far more pleasant dreams, dropping him into the nightmare of Gennie's foul morning mood. A tangle of long limbs and sheets, the youth tumbled from the bed and onto the cabin floor.

Composing his limbs enough to incline his chin on the rim of the mattress, the youth smiled a fair morning greeting, which turned to a troubled gaze at the sight of Gennie's pale features. He received a dark glare in return for his concern.

"To your feet, boy!" Gennie emitted the words with venom enough to send tremors through the man.

He snapped to a posture vaguely resembling a salute.

Gennie tore the sheets out of his grip revealing his narrow chest of sparsely haired flesh. A few short years ago, Gennie might have blushed, but no more. He was pretty and close enough to her age, but still too clumsy for the experience of a woman shaped by years of self-reliance on the sea.

Gennie would not allow her shaken state to betray her command, especially due to a swiftly evaporating nightmare.

"Retrieve your clothes. Get to the decks." Gennie was impressed at the rapidity mustered to make his way to the door, all the while pulling on breeches and boots. "Bring me our distance from Topolis!" Only a minor tremor remained to dance on the captain's well-trained tongue.

"And knock when you return!" she bellowed, vaulting a pillow at the closing door.

Only after the cabin door latched securely into place behind the man did Gennie allow her shoulders and controlled façade to drop. The last wisps of the strange vision shuddered off her small shoulders. Gennie swore she heard a final gasp of the voice and its anomalous question. Gennie swung her legs over the edge of the mattress. Her feet, dangling for only a moment over the high frame, slid down to meet the smooth planks of the floor. She gathered the sheet that had been her bedmate moments before and wrapped it around her like a toga. Pale toes with short, trimmed nails peeked from beneath the sheet draped and dragging in front of them. The sour feeling of a poorly begun morning and the hollowness left by a foolish dream melted with the aid of a blurry vision across the cluttered cabin. Gennie made her way to the amber-glass bottle propped within a nest of charts and maps on the broad oak desk. A bit of rum, even the remaining watered-down swill the supply had dwindled down to, would settle her mind. She snatched the bottle by its narrow neck and upended it over sleep-parched lips. The meager drizzle of pale, honey-toned liquid that dampened her tongue made her scowl.

"That is all?" she cursed. "Little whelp likely drank more of it than I. Would explain why he was so worthless last night."

Passing across the undersized cabin again, she flipped the bottle onto the disheveled expanse of bed. Captain's quarters though they were, Gennie's cabin was much smaller than most captains were privy to. It was a fair price in exchange for a ship as powerful and infamous as *Ecstasy*. The clutter of treasures, baubles, varied clothing from varied cultures, books in as many languages, maps, and charts, did not serve to make the room any more spacious. Walking past a wall, Gennie ran fingertips along a chain long enough to wrap around her hips twice over, heavy with burnished gold coins and bells. From a shelf of books, she plucked with gentle fingers a Venetian mask, plumed with peacock feathers and encrusted with faceted gems to match the plumage. With care not to muss the delicate workmanship, Gennie dusted off the piece and set it back less askew. She glanced at the door willing a few more minutes of peace before the stowaway returned from deck then she turned her attention out the small row of panes that looked onto the ocean behind. In small moments of quiet, she watched the wake waves in the surface of the deep blue.

Gennie's moment of meditation was shattered as her heel found a splinter in the otherwise smooth surface of the cabin floor. She let her body crumple into a cross-legged position. She breathed a slow steadying sigh and pulled the offending bit of wood from her foot. Waiting for the color to return to her face, Gennie leaned against the wall beneath the row of windows. "Shall we start this day with any more fair omens?" She rolled her deep brown eyes at the splinter before flinging it into the far corner among a cluster of wicker baskets.

On knees, Gennie crawled back to bed. She sifted through the tangle of sheets, pillows, and blankets. That boy, for all his inexperience and drunkenness, had kept her busy. She smiled wickedly at the singular pleasant memory the morning had to offer.

Stowaways were fair entertainment sometimes, willing to do most anything in exchange for completion of the free ride, instead of a swim in the open ocean.

"How many years ago were you offended by the same practices, Blackstrap?" she asked herself. She shrugged, "Things change."

Her tanned, olive-toned hand found the hem of a faded grey linen blouse, not hers. The youthful musk of her conquest would be a fond way to float through the day. She pulled the billowing garment over her head and continued to hunt for trousers. Her black silk pair would be the only ones in the folds of sheets. She buttoned the two small copper buttons and laced the front. Gennie bent to roll the cuffs to a more convenient length, tying the silk cord just below her knee. The legs of the trousers billowed over to fall mid-calf. Fishing knee-high, black, leather boots from under the bed, Gennie pulled them snuggly onto her feet; at least those fit properly. She pulled out a wide faded leather belt, adorned with pistol holster and gripped the brass handle of the single dueling pistol, checking the load. She picked up a pouch, empty of coin while aboard ship, small gold compass, and jade spyglass. Wrapping the belt at her waist, she slid the hooks and buckle to the last pair of vertical holes.

Her reflection did not boast that of the ideal pirate captain at a scant five-foot in height and a round face that defied her years. She raked the hand-carved ivory comb through a hip-length tousle of dark brown waves. Gennie missed the complex twists and braids that made maintenance of long hair much simpler. She would have to make time to have one among the harem dancers do the braiding.

Three sharp knocks at the cabin door turned Gennie's attention from the dark wood framed mirror. Turning back, she paused to frown once more at her bedraggled reflection, obscured by the wild mass of sun-and-sea-abused hair and broad-brimmed, black, leather cavalier hat. An unspoken apology rose with her gaze. She took the comb from the dressing table and tucked it into her belt, intent to endeavor to smooth her hair and braid it later.

Gennie strode across the room. Her sense of control returned as she turned alongside the dark wood shelf of books. Cautious fingers, with preservation of the books in mind, ran across the gold gilt or hand-scrawled titled spines of linen, leather, and silk. Pausing on a thick volume, she slid the wooden box with false binding from the ranks. She flipped open the latch and rested her eyes a moment on the small gold Medici pistol with hand tooled ivory grip wrapped in sea blue silk and resting in plush red velvet. Gennie secured the cover and latch. The box slid snugly back, unnoticeable among the books. She never left her cabin without ensuring the most important items, even ones hidden, were in their place. Gennie's eyes scanned the room once more as she swept the black coat from the chair back it rested across and onto her back.

"What?" She swung open the door of wood much lighter than her furnishings, expecting to be eye-to-eye with the sniveling owner of the shirt she had donned.

"What?" Gennie repeated with equivalent ferocity, this time elevating her gaze up roughly two feet.

"Expecting the little whelp returning for more abuse, Captain?" The sarcastic tone was more than perceptible. Had it come from any other than the thin pale lips of Gennie's first mate and most trusted confidant, it would have justified heavy reprimand.

Instead, Gennie merely smirked and rolled her shoulders, "Possibly." She swiveled her neck to glimpse around the tall slender man. "Did you drag him back for me? Truth be told, I think the boy relatively enjoyed his penalty."

"Aye, I imagine so." The first mate smiled with his pale green eyes down at his captain. "But no, I set the lad on other tasks."

"I'll have it from you then?" Gennie laid her index finger on the man's chest.

She waited for the familiar rise of thin, pale, brown eyebrows, a look that, due to years of practice, interpreted with ease the duality in every utterance from this always cunning and once innocent French girl turned pirate captain. He hoped for the more pleasurable meanings of Gennie's words, but knew better.

"Our position, sir." She turned her finger and tapped him on the chin, yet another innuendo he would smile and make note of. "I am referring to the ship, of course. What did you imagine I meant, Mr. Marrick?"

He shook his head, knowing she knew, but would never admit. "Two days." The statement made Gennie beam. "If we stay our course and the winds stay fair."

"No more?" Gennie pressed.

Marrick gave a slight incline of his head in response to Gennie's query. "Good." A broad grin spread across her round face displaying one chipped front tooth in an otherwise glittering smile.

For five years, Gennie explored seas and islands in search of select acquaintances remembered from her adolescence as most capable to be a trusted and responsible crew. Topolis, she anticipated, would be where she would find the last. Within the week, she would complete her extensive quest. Then, only fresh exploit would beckon her *Ecstasy*.

Gennie stepped into the doorframe forcing Marrick's position to shift against the wall and permit Gennie course. For a moment, their bodies caressed one another, furnishing memories all but as close as what once was, and could have been, a calm and picturesque future.

Chapter 2

The highlights of every destination brought enchantment to Solange and welcome reprieve from the doldrums of ship life and the loss of her family. A young woman unaccustomed to life beyond the walls of her father's vast estate, her naïve spirit and insatiable curiosity did not give pause to wander into port town streets at any hour alone. Solange could never tell where she had turned or how far she had gone when roving. Even aboard ship she would become mislaid. A step down wrong alleys caused at least the occasional ruthless run-ins. Ill-fated cabin boys were sent to shadow or to locate the habitually lost adolescent. Mercifully, after losing coin and small trinkets on hand, Solange returned to the ship.

Marrick had been the one to hit upon a means to keep the girl from wandering and to establish some defense if she did. He had not anticipated the pretext to grow to be so agreeable to him as well.

Solange's novice footing wobbled the log she balanced on. She recovered for a moment, then, and fell into the lengthy arms of the first mate of *Lenore*. She hid her blush at being so close to the young officer with a fuming outburst of frustration.

"You need to focus, Sol," Marrick laughed and deposited the girl on the log to attempt the balancing act once more.

"Arrêtez de me soulever comme je suis une poupée de chiffon." Solange prepared herself on the balance beam moving with caution into the stance Marrick had explained on so many occasions and that Solange had observed him teaching others aboard ship.

Marrick laughed. "In English, ma chere. Don't be forgettin' the other bit of training that you are workin' on."

The girl's jaw set, she pressed her teeth and lips to cage unladylike retorts.

"Stop placing me about, I am no doll to be lifted here and there." She pointed and the gesture took her balance for a breath.

"Poppet, if you stop fallin' like one, I'll stop treatin' you like one." Marrick laughed again, a short sound with a gasp and sputtering snigger, to watch the girl regain her footing.

Solange sighed in consigned aggravation. "Et do not name me poppet, or Sol, or any other name but mine." Her brow knit as she controlled her temper and used it to focus her poise and position her blade. "Sol sounds of some sea beast or insect."

"Oh, of course, Mademoiselle Solange de LeRenard," Marrick bowed, an awkward gesture at his height, with a flourish of his hand. "I also suppose I cannot christen you my little fox," he winked.

Solange flushed. She veiled her embarrassment once again in feigned fury and leveled her slender blade at Marrick's eyes. Marrick positioned with back to the beam, his feet remaining firmly planted on level ground and the tilt of his blade level with Solange's.

At scarcely five feet, standing on the beam made Solange roughly equivalent to Marrick's six-foot-eight inch stature. In contrast, it did naught to assist her arm's reach.

"Cette pas lutte equitable," she sulked. "Your arms are two times mine. C'est impossible I reach to you without being struck."

Marrick shook his head and smirked at the girl. "There's always a way. And, what, are you assuming pirates and thieves are runts like you?"

Solange put a hand on her hip, letting her guard down. Marrick waved his fingers beckoning Solange to make her move.

"More likely most will be my size, or better!" He lunged at her.

Solange caught Marrick's blade with hers, though only just, before the blade caught her. Her feet and legs quivered on the beam, but she did not fall. Her poise, improving since the beginnings of her instruction, still perturbed her to be required to stand so uncomfortably.

"Et pour quoi must I stand on this stupide log!" She stomped the beam, her anger quickly replaced by shock as she rebalanced.

"Stability. To train you to become as small a target as possible. Not a big deal for you though. And," he tapped his temple with the flat of the sword, "so you might have an ability to reach my head," Marrick stated.

"I do have this balance and stability. The court is expected to know the dances, and I am well trained." Solange offered the excuse with her head held high and hands on hips.

"Ships ain't stable, poppet. Dancin' with a blade is far different than prancin' on a ballroom floor. And fightin' is sure not done in pretty shoes." Marrick gestured with the tip of his blade at the space just below the log. An almost child-size pair of pale-green leather slippers lay carefully discarded within Solange's reach.

Solange sighed. She glanced at her bare toes. Her feet were looking more like those of a poor sailor than a daughter of the court every day.

Her training from the first mate of *Lenore* was vexing, though she knew the man meant well. He had taken her as his charge almost upon meeting, treating her as one of the crew and as a little sister. He was typically chief in the search party for her when she vanished for any span of time. With no kin left to her, Solange was comforted to have someone to depend on.

"Why do you not teach me when we are on the ship?" She knocked his blade away and moved into the open gap nearly touching Marrick's shoulder before having to retreat from his return assault. Solange recovered her footing with more ease than prior maneuvers.

"Because, poppet, if the captain saw how badly you fight, he would have you off the ship at the next port for sure." Marrick thrust. "A woman aboard is bad luck enough." The blades hissed against one another.

"Je peux tirer." Solange back-stepped and countered. She curled her fingers as if to hold a pistol. Marrick could not contradict that the young woman had proficiency with a musketoon. He had snickered at her for even lifting the firearm until he had seen her fire and regretted the mocking when the ball whispered passed his ear to strike her intended target of the rum bottle in his hand. Since that argument he had focused only on training her with a blade and staying clear of her quiet temper if cannons or pistols were about.

"Blades don't run out of bullets," Marrick parried, "nor are they affected by a little water."

Solange slapped the blade aside with the back of her wrist of her open hand, "Oui, but I do love the noise." Continuing the movement, she kicked one leg off the log and sliced crossways with the blade. She halted her revolution with blade poised at Marrick's ear.

The young man's eyes were wide. "I heard that one." He put a hand up to push the blade away.

"Blades do rust and weaken after some time in salt water." Solange worked to restrain the smirk forcing its way to her lips. "Nothing is infallible, monsieur." She allowed herself a wide grin at her obvious triumph.

10

Marrick returned to a ready stance. "Dance moves don't count. And, you talk too much. You should be letting your sword speak for you."

"You are the one who said there is always a way." Solange prepared to clash again. "This is my way," she shrugged.

"That little trick won't work twice," Marrick advised.

Solange shrugged, "Maybe not on you, maybe not today, but it may work again." She leveled her blade over his shoulder and nodded for him to look.

The flag in the distance alerted the close of their practice session.

"Is there anything you are not trying to be a master at?" Marrick tapped the girl's blade away and positioned to begin again.

"I do not have to be a master at anything, but I do enjoy many things now that I am able." Solange tapped her opponent's blade with her own.

"Enough for today." He stated as if the close of session were his idea, and not the call back to the ship.

Marrick put a hand out to assist Solange down from the beam.

The handle of the sword met his presented hand instead. Solange smirked and stepped down from her perch. Marrick shook his head. The lady was fast becoming something more to contend with.

"You can behave like a lady now and then," Marrick advised. "You will hurt a man's feelings and make yourself impossible to wed if you're not careful."

Solange rolled her eyes. "I am not fool enough to think I am still worth anything without land or title. There are no rules for a worthless woman."

Marrick read the sorrow behind the words, but knew better than to note it. "Aye, you are right. No man wants a little whelp like you." Marrick danced beyond the girl's reach and sprinted in the direction of the harbor.

Solange gave chase, but with three of her steps being worth one of Marrick's, she knew there would be no expectation to catch the man. Marrick kept the chase on, always laughing, just a bit shy of the girl falling from exhaustion.

Solange swung a diminutive fist and connected with Marrick's rib. He stared down at her. "Oh, ow, the pain!" He feigned, gripping the side opposite her strike. "I will give you that I deserved that, but next time," he paused to gesture, "try aiming for my face. If you can reach."

Solange was not amused. She lingered only long enough to recover her breath before storming away leaving Marrick laughing.

"Are you going to forget everything I taught you by the next port?" He inquired once he caught up to the girl.

Solange jogged to keep pace, struggling to remain in advance of Marrick as they drew near the ship. "Évidement non." She did not raise an eye to the man.

Solange's mood altered as *Lenore* came into sight. No matter how many times she witnessed the ship, it still struck her with wonder. The caravel towered in the dockyard, and though the sails were drawn up and gunwales closed, Solange could see *Lenore's* full splendor when in bloom. Solange and Marrick said naught until the gangway, she admiring *Lenore* and he admiring the girl's appreciation for the ship he called home. Marrick seized her arm as they reached the foot of the plank.

"You are getting pretty good, even though I tease you." He looked down at the girl. "I almost think you can save your own ass if trouble arises."

Solange beamed, "Pretty good. Hmmm. Je peux l'accepter. Not that ever I expected your assistance. Maybe it is you who will need saving instead."

She shook the hand from her arm and left Marrick on the dock as she scuttled up the gangplank. He trailed after a moment and glancing down the way they had come, checked behind to see if any stragglers might be on the approach.

Marrick surveyed the busy deck of *Lenore*, noting any that might be slacking off.

"Marrick!" The captain called out from the access to his cabin.

"Aye captain." Marrick dispensed the swords to a passing crewman and met the captain halfway.

"You have been teaching the girl and feel obligated as you are the best swordsman I have." He held a hand up before Marrick could protest. "Skills aside, there are more pressing duties aboard ship for a man of your rank. Have another teach her in your place." The older man put a hand on the younger's shoulder. "I did not choose a man so young as a first mate to have a skirt-chasing doe-eyed fool as my second in command. You will speak to the daughter of the late Monsieur de LeRenard no more than any other passenger or crew on this ship or you will speak to her not at all."

"Captain, aye. She needs a proper instructor," Marrick sought to explain. The captain held up a hand to silence him. Though taller than the captain by half a head, Marrick still looked up to the man with respect. He would not contravene the order, though it pained him.

"She'll wander if she's bored," Marrick reasoned.

"Pass her off to one of your most trusted. I will allow the choice to be yours, but you will not waste time on her that should be mine." His tone was firm, though not heartless. "I do agree that giving her lessons is less trouble than searching every port city for her foolish hide. Bless my dear late friend, but he did leave the most willful of his heirs."

Marrick concurred. He turned away to witness Solange bounding up the steps from the deck below. She had changed her attire to more ladylike skirts, blouse, and vest, her long chestnut hair pulled into a neat twist at the nape of her neck. Aboard ship she was under the captain's orders to behave as much like her former station mandated feasible. In particular when other passengers were with them, to look as though she were a member of the crew could mean ruin for his business. She was not to tell any other traveler her surname, however, in case the church still sought to eradicate the Huguenot offspring of the Ile de Roi aristocracy.

"Bonjour, captain. Marrick," Solange curtsied.

Her salutation lingered longer on Marrick than the captain. Marrick smiled at the girl, but a glance over his shoulder at the captain advised that his latest order commenced immediately.

"Good day, Mademoiselle." Marrick tipped his hat to Solange. He saluted the captain. "I have your leave, captain, to attend to duties."

Solange stared quizzically as Marrick strode past without so much as a second glance.

"Good day to you, Solange," the captain greeted.

Solange smiled at the captain but turned a second time to follow Marrick with her eyes. Her mind retraced the day in speculation of whether she had done something wrong since their return to the ship, though she could not imagine what. There was always jest between the pair, but it never left ill feelings.

"Marrick," she called out before looking to the captain for some motive for the man's actions.

"Solange?" The captain's comforting expression concealed something, though Solange could not place it. "Have you thought much about my advice to you? And a name to be called while aboard my ship, should any new passengers ask it of you."

"Evidement," Solange replied but her gaze returned to Marrick's direction a moment more.

"Young men are fickle, child." The captain caught the girl's chin in his hand. "You will learn this with age. Now come along. If you are to earn your space on my ship we must teach you some things."

Solange looked at the captain's arm as he offered her to take it. She looked into the man's eyes for the answers he held from her. He smiled down at her. The captain escorted her to the helm.

"Our heading is here, Solange. Would you like to see?" The captain offered her the rolled map in his palm.

Taking the map, she carefully unrolled it onto the table at the helm. Beyond the words in French, it was scribbles to her. Solange noted the markings on the chart, trying to learn to read the scrawling but having limited luck.

"I am sorry, captain, much of this is English, which I have learned to speak as well as most but can only read un peu." His broad hat shadowed his expression.

"You will have much more time without others to distract you," he replied.

It did take time, but Solange was a diligent student and quicker with reading than she expected. The captain was a patient man as was his navigator. With the aid of the two men, Solange learned the skills and uses for the tools required to be a meager navigator at the least. It was the only position aboard ship the captain would allow her since it required little heavy labor and much time hidden away from other passengers.

By chance alone, in most cases, she found new routes to busy ports.

She did not see Marrick for more than a few moments of each voyage, and not at all if they were docked. She continued some lessons with Jacob, who was a close friend of the first mate, but a mediocre fighter, and not nearly so much a joy to be near. After a time, Solange grew acutely aware of Marrick's avoiding her. She lost interest in fighting Jacob and remained in the archives, poring over maps and books. Her vision often blurred by the sudden change in her friend's mood toward her but never when anyone was around to see.

"'Hoy." Solange looked up from the map she was puzzling.

Marrick was standing in the doorway. She did not smile and turned her eyes back to the desk.

"May I assist you?" Solange replied curtly.

"Your English is better," Marrick noted. "I've been listening to you relay our headings to the navigator and captain. "Didn't think you could even read in your native tongue; now, you read English."

Solange glared at the man before turning toward the bookshelves. "Is there something you require?"

"I'm beginning not to care about the order to ignore you." Marrick stepped into the room.

Solange refused to look up as she turned back to the maps she was surveying.

"Hey," Marrick put a hand on the map, blocking it from Solange's view, "I'm talking here."

"And I am not listening here." Her manner calm, Solange turned away from the map and pulled another book from the shelf behind her.

Marrick glowered at the girl. He turned his back to lean against the desk, both hands on the maps. Solange dropped the oversized atlas on the man's splayed hands.

"Damn it, woman!" Marrick hissed and rescued his hand. He shook out his fingers and scowled. "I owe you one for that. Not that you will pay it."

"Now that you will no longer be around me, you cannot fight me either." Solange shrugged.

Marrick shook his head and made a face. He brought a

finger level with the girl's eyes. "Listen here, now, I didn't have choice in that."

Solange crossed her arms and stared at the hand in her face.

"I am here now," Marrick offered turning his hand out. "Did you miss me?"

"Non." Solange set her hands on her hips. She pouted only a moment before continuing to her tasks. Solange returned the atlas to its place on the shelf, having finished with her need for it.

"What the? Come on, Sol. You don't mean that." Marrick put his hands up. "Look. It's me."

Sol tilted her head. She might always be tested by Marrick's sword, but her wit was sharper than his. She could wait and make him suffer a bit in return for ignoring her for so long.

"Come on now, don't be mad. You're not really mad with me." Marrick moved across the room. "You can't stay mad at me, ever."

"I can and I will." Solange backed away.

"Well there's only one thing for me to do with you!" Marrick lunged, and before Solange had a chance to move and counter, she was hoisted onto the man's shoulder, head towards the floor and room spinning. She beat her fists against his back and squealed in protest as Marrick laughed at the girl's suffering.

"Tu me déposeres, monsieur! Tout de suite!" Solange commanded slipping into her native tongue.

"Ah ah! In English, little fox. You've been doin' so well," Marrick teased.

"Put me down!" Solange kicked.

At the order Marrick swept her off his shoulder, flipped the girl back to her feet and set her on the floor. He was grinning wildly at his victory. Solange stumbled about the room, arms seeking something to steady her in her dizzied state.

"Je te deteste." she hissed.

Marrick laughed. "In English, please," he choked out between hiccups of laughter.

"I do hate you!" Solange stomped her foot and nearly fell from her lack of balance.

Marrick roared with laughter. "Oh come on, poppet," Marrick knelt down, almost at the same height as Solange and held her arms so she would not fall. "You love me."

"I do not," Solange pouted, but her anger was subsiding with the return of her stability.

Marrick held the girl's shoulders while the last of her dizzy spell subsided. He released her slowly as she seemed steady. His eyes glittered, watching to be certain she did not fall, or strike at him. Solange knocked his arms away.

"Why are you here now, if you are under orders?" Solange returned to her maps.

"Someone had to come down to get the new charts," Marrick grinned at his perceived slyness. "Come on. You know me. I can con anyone; just takes more time an' plannin' with some."

Solange shook her head but smiled. "Why do I allow you to behave so foolishly?"

"You wouldn't have me any other way," Marrick shrugged.

Solange gathered the charts, ignoring his teasing words. Marrick watched the girl double check that she had everything she needed and followed her around the cabin.

Solange sighed. The scowl on her lips faded to a small smile.

"You've kept busy without me?" Marrick moved to reconnect with the young woman.

"I have." Solange dumped her supplies into a folio.

"Tell me all about it." Marrick smiled, "Tonight." He bent, surprising Solange with a sudden, brief kiss on her cheek.

"I do not like my new teacher," Solange said as she paused

in the doorway. She glanced at Marrick a moment more before continuing into the walkway.

Marrick laughed, "You're not supposed to like him. You're supposed to hit him with all you've got."

"I liked you," Solange remarked after a moment.

"That's why you always lost," Marrick shrugged. "You held back. And 'cause I'm just that good."

When Solange did not respond he continued, "Captain was wrong to part us. And, I knew you hated Jacob." Marrick grinned, "Hit 'im good for me, aye, poppet." He mussed her neatly ribbon-bound hair.

Solange sighed, "Aye, hit him I will." A smirk played across her lips, "But I will be picturing you and your comment that I hold back when striking."

Solange brushed ahead with her armload of charts. There were other reasons the captain had separated them, she knew, but she said nothing. She had hidden her emotion well enough to at least keep the friendship. She would not be so weak again.

Lenore's luck ran out that fine fall evening. In taking a narrow route in the straits, she was cornered.

At the sight of the pirate vessel, the crew prepared for battle. Solange had never seen the full power of *Lenore* rolled into position. The caravel had always been a beauty on the ocean, elegant and majestic like a fine lady. The thunder of the fire-breathing cannons echoed with each shot. Solange watched over the rails the horror she had brought the ship and her friends into.

Through the chaos, Marrick appeared at her side. He handed her the sword she had only ever practiced with. The look in his eyes told her this lesson was no game.

"I don't want to see you use this unless you have to." Marrick's cool eyes bore into Solange. "Get below decks. Stay with your books and maps."

Marrick grabbed a scurrying cabin boy and commanded him to make Solange look as much like one of them and least like a girl as they could.

The cabin boy grabbed Solange by the arm to lead her away. She shook the boy off.

"I am sorry," Solange cried. "This is the fault of my navigations. I will not run from a fight I brought us into."

Marrick set his jaw. "The navigator didn't even look at your map this time, Sol. You're a piss poor navigator, but you're not stupid, and you've the luck of a devil. Like me."

Solange was confused.

"The captain's dead, Sol." Marrick's eyes worked not to betray his loss. "We were set up."

Marrick nodded to the cabin boy. He swept Solange onto his shoulder and bolted down the steps into the lower levels of the ship.

The ruse succeeded. When the vessel was taken, Solange stood with the men. Dressed in ill-fitting blouse and trousers, a shabby hat hiding her face, her hair hacked, unevenly to her shoulders, she was not dealt with, as a woman would have been.

Surprise came to all aboard when Solange was asked, as all the others had been, if she would join the pirates or join the sea. She replied with an unfaltering, "Aye, Captain."

She aided the pirates in the transfer of the goods, and took all of the maps, tools, and books for herself. Nothing was left that could be taken. Guns, supplies, food and water, the pirates meant not to waste time or bullets on the crew, only to leave them adrift to starve slowly or be taken by one another through cannibalism or madness.

Solange meant to leave *Lenore* a boon, though, as an apology for what she felt was her fault. Even if she had not been the one to direct her friends into the tragedy, she had not known enough to help them avoid it either. Carefully scrawled inside the secret stores cabinet, a place she knew Marrick would look for food and supplies, Solange left a simple map depicting the fastest route to the nearest port, the one last chance she had to prove her navigational skills. It would become her mark. For every ship the pirates raided, she would take all of the maps, logs, and information, and leave the crew with her map. This first map, though, was the most important.

When the pirates marched the handful of turncoats, most that had already given their allegiance and were members of the plot to take *Lenore*, across the plank to the black-sailed galleon, Solange was among them.

She did not look at the crew of *Lenore*, her family for her time at sea, as she marched past.

"Sol," Marrick hissed, "don't do this, girl."

Solange paused for only a moment, "When we meet again, you will not call me Sol like an insect."

Chapter 3

Gennie broke the moment with another step, "I will see how fair these winds are then."

The captain swayed with each step through the open deck strewn with net hammocks, some still heavy with a sleeping sailor. Gennie stretched a little, her body still waking from her strange night, and reached, prodding into waking a few sailors she recognized as those late to duties. Personal items in trunks, satchels, and barrels, crowded the floor spaces surrounding structural beams. The low ceilings and wall-less lower decks, save for the captain's cabin and a handful of other created rooms, made for a communal and trusting atmosphere on *Ecstasy*. She smiled as she admired her crew that through cultural, social, gender, and linguistic diversity had become a strange class of family. She made her way up to the deck while Marrick followed close behind, his long legs begging to move at a more reasonable pace than the diminutive officer's stride.

The crew of *Ecstasy* was a motley bunch, as Gennie liked it. She had no qualms about the age or gender of a crewmember so long as he or she could do the job set upon him or her. Each crew man had a history that had brought Gennie to seek him or her out as trusted crew. The stories, that's what villagers did not get to see or hear when they think of pirates, men and women who, created by a life that held far less freedom, are lost at sea, trying to find treasure and fill the voids left on land

The sun struck Gennie's hat shadowing her face as she stepped onto the top deck. Cool sea air fluttered the feathers in the upturned brim. She rested a hand on the top of her head as she inclined her gaze to gauge the fullness of the sails. Battened curtains of pale green billowed in the steady wind. At least the day was as clear and the wind as blessed as Marrick described, Gennie thought. She made her way across the expansive deck of the junk, taking in the morning's bustle across the ship. *Ecstasy* had seen neither land nor passing ship in a week's stretch. Not even a rumor of other pirates had whispered from any of the small islands they had supplied from last. There was little to do save for preparations to make port at Topolis. Most of the crew enjoyed the calm winds, fishing, and dancing. working at menial tasks, whiling away or counting coin, or trade before making landfall.

Gennie drew the delicate jade-and-copper-clad spyglass always kept with her from her coat pocket. Yet again shaking off the memory of the strange dream and the vision of a ship she could not decide to run to or away from, the captain put the device to her eye.

"Empty," She reported to no one, though Marrick still cast a shadow. Relief or remorse, she could not tell which, released a sigh from her lips.

"Aye," the man responded. "It's been dull this past month." Marrick put a hand on her shoulder. "I know you, Sol. Something's been on your mind. More than quiet waters. You know I'd do what it takes to shake your worry, but I also know to trust it."

Gennie did not reproof the man for the pet name she thought long forgotten.

"Ennui is not my concern, Marrick. You are right. There will be scores of ships and ports to plunder where we are sailing after our stop in Topolis," Gennie assured the first mate. "But to see no other ship at all, this close? There is a thing to make my sus-

24

picions rise. Aye, trust the instinct, but I wish I had a better reason why my dreams haunt me and my eyes beg to search sea and charts with such frequency."

* * *

Your armies have secured every harbor, sultana." The general bowed in the presence of his ruler.

He raised his eyes to meet hers. The sultana rested languid among her concubine, those who remained after the korsana made off with the others.

M'nef Sheilk was a woman unaccustomed being denied anything she desired, and most often her desires were orders, disobeyed only with heavy consequence. For five years, however, the sultana raged over one order given and not followed. The order was to a young impetuous pirate woman.

Concubines closest to the throne shifted back and prepared to duck if the need arose.

"Very much at my pleasure, sir, very much," the sultana grinned. "I want that Djinn bottled." The sultana's rage was at a simmer. She held her manner controlled with much effort.

She waved long fingers in dismissal to the messenger and leaned on the arms of her throne. Scowling at the memory of the pirate woman. "I will have that woman back here with my concubines and dancers. I will have my property back, I will have that dragon ship, and I will have AdeebA Korsana's head as a treasure box if she disobeys me." She hissed as she allowed her slender body to sink into the deep purple silk pillows surrounding her.

"Are you certain it is wise to bring the korsana back to the palace alive, my queen?" the sultana's minister asked. "It would be just as well to have your soldiers bring her head to you on a gold platter with your dancers and concubines following on chains of gold."

The sultana sat as though listening to the minister, but the woman's words ignored him. She decided the day AdeebA Korsana escaped, stole from her, and made her look a fool, she would see the woman face to face again. The desire was not to ensure the pirate made good on her word, but to torture the korsana with her own hand for blatant disobedience.

"I will see AdeebA Korsana breathing." M'nef petted the hair of the concubine beside her. "Perhaps there is a chance the woman can be broken still. She may yet be a bit of entertainment as was my original plan."

* * *

"A good captain behaves with vigilance. You've learnt from others mistakes." Marrick bent to be eye to eye with Gennie. "And your own."

Gennie collapsed the spyglass and, returning it to her pocket, turned her head to face Marrick. "But some warning beyond instinct and paranoia would be considerably welcome if I am taking my crew into more trouble than we can navigate."

Gennie's dark eyes searched the hazel of Marrick's for some answer. They had seen much together and more apart. She trusted his instinct as much as he did hers. The light she did see after a moment locked in thought was not one she cared to pursue with her mind in turmoil.

"I hope I am not interrupting anything, my lady captain." The jovial impish glint of grey eyes drew Gennie's gaze from Marrick, "But my ears did hear the word navigate and were bid to draw me to the sound almost as well as a glint of treasure draws my hands."

Marrick, knocked aside by the hip of Maggie Pye, did his

best not to make his annoyance apparent. Maggie's broad smile shoved aside any dread Gennie could ever feel.

"Good morning, Mademoiselle Pye. I am pleased your eavesdropping skills have not tapered. You save me the stroll to locate you."

Maggie's grin broadened to an expansive and impish width. "Aye, indeed, and we are well aware how lost you might become, so I am pleased as well to save you such a stroll."

Gennie draped an arm over Maggie's shoulder and around Marrick's waist, lips curling in a half grin at the jab. "I will make note of that compliment, Miss Pye. I hear from Marrick we are doing well. Let us walk as we discuss this, so I will not become mislaid while on my rounds."

Maggie retrieved a map from her ample cleavage as they ambled arm-in-arm across the deck with Marrick a step after.

"Aye, indeed we have, belle." She shook the creases from the document.

Gennie shot the navigator a narrow fleeting look.

"Captain," a furtive beam brushed across the woman's countenance as she nodded.

Gennie could not contain her amusement at the woman. The beauty was more a sister to her than a crewman. The navigator was one of the earliest with her from the time when the only craft Gennie could dub her own was a skiff, and was foremost on her mind to locate upon acquiring *Ecstasy*.

"Today is not the day to be calling me a beauty, Maggie." Gennie massaged her temples beneath the brim of her hat.

"Too much to drink, is it, captain, or just too much of that young drink that stowed away on our last stop?" Maggie joked. She paused, "But no, I think it is more than that, but more my captain will not say."

Gennie muttered and rolled her eyes. "Maggie, too well you

know me, too well. You will hear more of my concerns than most on this vessel, but there are secrets I have kept and will keep even from you, ma belle. Be assured that anything that might be of use will come to you directly from my lips and none other.”

She took leave from looking into Maggie's eyes to survey the maps.

“No headaches, at least as far as voyage is concerned. This route will take us through clear waters,” Maggie guaranteed her captain.

“Every route has taken us through clear waters, Maggie.” Gennie stared at the chart as if it would proclaim some answer.

Maggie could only shrug. When the maps did not provide, Gennie looked to her again. She, too, was at a loss. Her maps and charts offered her no more than had she been a novice. Superstitious as she was, she moved not to provoke the fates to temptation by questioning them, however, and counted the peace encountered as a blessing.

“Come, now,” Maggie set a hand on the captain's shoulder, “how about allowing the trusted navigator to give an order?”

Gennie looked at the woman with raised brow. “Bien, your order then, Miss Pye?”

Maggie slid a narrow gold-and-amber-decorated flask from her hip, “A bit of your namesake to cure what ails ye?”

A smile crept across Gennie's lips despite her worries, “And I say it again, Miss Pye, too well you know me. Too well.”

Gennie took a long pull from the flask and held it out to share.

Marrick made to take the flask after Gennie's turn, eager as always for a taste of Blackstrap. Maggie snatched the bottle from his reach and shook her finger at the man, “Ladies first. Have some courtesy.” Maggie's scolding tone fell on Marrick's ears but rolled off his back.

“Aye and you have always been a lady,” Marrick rolled his

28

eyes, "either of you."
  The pair exchanged a knowing glance at one another.

Chapter 4

Solange slammed the heavy mug onto the table. Her eyes flicked to the three large, globelike bottles of rum, still full, then flicked to the woman opposite her at the table.

"I am not sure who is paying for all we have so far consumed, mademoiselle, mais I could consume more as long as it is not coming from my pocket." She leaned on the bottle in her other hand as she slurred out the words.

"Aye. Well, pretty, the coin is not coming from my purse so drink away." Maggie set her mug down after another swallow.

The two had entered the small Jamaican tavern separately and with separate intentions. Quickly, though, they found common interest and distraction from their intended tasks. Two bottles later on Maggie's side and four on Solange's, the pair had outlasted every sailor and farmer in the room.

"Qu'est-ce que c'est que we are drinking encore, ma chere?" She was slipping rapidly into her native tongue, a sure sign Solange was beginning to feel the effects of the alcohol.

"Rum. More specifically, Blackstrap molasses rum." Maggie swirled another bottle in her hand. "It is soon to be all that is in your blood at the rate you drink, small one."

Solange scowled, "And you as well, non, Miss Pye? You have had near as much as I, and I will hear no more of my size being the reason for my stopping."

Maggie laughed and poured another round. She, too, was beginning to enjoy herself a bit too much. The woman had long ago marinated in every form of drink and could handle any poison and more than most others.

This small sailor girl, however, was matching Maggie better than any pirate. Where Solange slipped into proper French and improper behavior, however, Maggie became more the lady of courtesy and less the thief she really was.

"I am not here for the drink, my small lady," Maggie whispered as she filled Solange's mug.

"Je sais," Solange leaned over her mug.

Maggie was a touch taken aback by the response, but looking in the wide eyes of the girl, she brushed the comment away as the talk of a drunken wench.

"You are here for," Solange tilted her head in the direction of a foppish youth with an overfed appearance.

Maggie's eyes flicked to the youth and back to the woman in front of her. "Him?"

Solange grinned and drank deep from her mug, draining enough to see her partner through the clear base. "Not him," her head wobbled as she worked to focus Maggie's reflection through the cup base, "his rings."

"You are very perceptive, small lady." Maggie hid her shock in sarcasm.

This strange young woman was beginning to amaze Maggie. Solange was equally intrigued. She was fast becoming glad that the captain had given her leave, through negligence, to take the skiff of *Lenore* as her own, at least while they traveled among the isles of the new world. Solange had not met many on the island that could be considered interesting, but Maggie Pye was making up for that.

"Je suis," Solange smirked, "et tu have an eye for all that glitters, belle."

"Very perceptive indeed," Maggie noted, "It is like a curse: I am drawn to sparklies like the compass to true north," Maggie's eyes sparkled.

"I have been watching you." Solange put the neck of the bottle beside her eye. "You have tabled every man with coin, pocketed his treasures, and floored me with your skill. So how is it you intend to obtain the trinkets to which you are so drawn from a man whose gluttony is not for drink, but food," Solange leaned on her elbows toward the woman.

Solange admired the curve of the woman's full lips and the glint in her mellow grey eyes. She took notice of the twisted gold spirals that held chestnut curls in place and the string of gold discs spaced by deep red-orange stones that circled around the rich cream flesh. Even the burgundy corset that hugged the woman, emphasizing already well-molded curves, was shot through with swirls and streaks of thread of gold.

"You are very observant indeed, small one." Solange made note of the sound made when Maggie shifted her position to lean closer over the table. The slide of coins unmistakable, though muffled by the red velvet pouches dangling intermittently at Maggie's hips.

There was no doubt the woman knew treasure. She could possibly smell the purity in metal. The glint of precious stone, an easy thing for her to spot from any distance. Yes, Solange was beginning to believe, could be led to sparklies, as Maggie termed them, via a force like a compass magnet. To believe she could just walk up to the fop and convince him to hand over his wealth, no chance.

"If I tell you, you might decide it a good idea for you to try, miss," Maggie whispered.

Solange choked back a laugh, "No. Non, ma belle. This day I am not after anything to fill my pockets. I seek to fill my soul and drain more than a few bottles."

Maggie tilted her head.

"Rum, tu dit, cette la? This island has the best drink I have ever come to know, and it is true the best according pirates and sailors." Solange breathed, and Maggie smelled her point well enough.

"You hope to take a few bottles along for the next trip?" Maggie was catching on to the ways in which Solange worked.

"Aye. A few of the best," Solange pointed to the bottles closest to the fop Maggie had her eye on.

"So we have the same target for differing reasons," Maggie gathered the plot this seeming innocent was hatching.

"What do you say, belle, to an arrangement to the benefit of both toi et moi?" Solange batted her lashes and knit her hands to rest her chin.

Maggie's look was enough to count as an agreement to the partnership. The pair downed one more mug after a toast to their imminent success to seal the deal.

A curt nod to one another, the women stood from their benches in unison. They swung one leg at a time over the benches and swaggered to close the distance to their target.

Inches from their prey, "Wench!" Maggie blurted as Solange tripped over the leg of a chair and fell into the woman.

Maggie pushed the girl off and onto her feet again.

"Chien," Solange shot back, venom in her tone. She swung and missed.

Maggie returned the swing, circled, and bumped the fop's table.

The fop looked up, too late, to a pair of balled fists in his face. Solange shook out the impact.

The man rolled in his seat before his weight toppled him off balance and onto the floor with a shuddering crash.

Solange's eyes went wide complementing a drunken smile of shock. She looked at Maggie, uncertain what to do next.

34

Maggie smiled, but only for a breath. It was barely enough of an expression for Solange to notice with no chance any others in the bar saw.

"You have knocked him out, ye depraved French tart!" Maggie railed at Solange, their faces inches apart.

Solange could smell the rum on the thief's tongue. She blinked her minute amount of sobriety back after.

Maggie bent to help the swelling fop to his feet, each of his hands in each of hers.

"I? Mais non! C'est ton travaille," Solange hissed back. She grabbed the pair of bottles from the table beside the fallen man.

A bottle in each hand, Solange approached the backing Maggie.

"Whoa now, pretty?" Maggie's hands went first to her chest, crossing to ward off the drunken devil child closing on her.

The pair moved toward the door. Maggie's hands pushed at sailors seated along a length of bench. Men hardly sober enough to know where they were no less moved out of harm's path.

Solange swung the bottles high, clear of any harm that might have come from a more steady hand.

Patrons of the bar, the few still sober and untouched by Maggie's drinking plots, walled the women in but allowed them to move in whatever direction they chose to dance. It was not about ending the fight between the women, but following with the best view of what might occur in the next moment. Sailors did so love a good wench war.

Solange swung the bottle in her right hand. Maggie leaned, though unnecessarily, out of the bottle's path. She continued to be backed toward the main entrance to the tavern. Solange swung wild, with her right then her left, forcing the crowd around and behind to fan out and give more than ample space.

The pair managed a path onto the front porch of the bar. Cool air struck the women somewhat more sober. Solange glanced around, throwing into another wide sweep with the bottles. She broke into a run when she saw Maggie stumble, step back, regain her footing, and pause in the street for a moment.

"I have you now!" Solange whooped.

Another moment and Maggie spun out of range of the swinging bottles yet again and was off at a run in the direction of the beach.

"So you say, small one!" A manic laugh escaped Maggie's lips.

Solange gave chase with a raucous howl and screech, bottles swirling in her hands.

The patrons and owner of the tavern were left wordless. They watched the pair gallop over the ridge and out into the darkness.

"Thieves!" the fop had regained some consciousness and sense.

He slumped at the far end of the room, all eyes on his plump, brocade-wrapped form. The man held a pale lace kerchief to his swelling cheek, the side that Maggie had struck darkening much more than the side Solange had connected. His fingers were bare.

"Those bottles were meant for the governor! Someone fetch them back!" The youth demanded of the staring crowd.

The crowd looked out into the dark beyond the fires of the porch. A few looked back at the fop. Most smiled and shook their heads.

"No business of ours, mate, if ye can't handle a woman or two on your own merit." The barkeep laughed until reality dawned on him as well. "Oi, wait a minute." He looked at the table where the women had been seated. Eight drained bottles of his best rum sat empty beside a pair of plates void of the food delivered on them. The pewter mugs were nowhere to be seen. Same for the knives.

"Damned wenches!" the big man took both fists to the heavy bar sending a crack the length of the wood. "Bloody thieves!"

At this point, many of the patrons were patting down their own pockets. Sure as the sun, any that Maggie had touched on her path to the door had not a thing of value on them.

Following what transpired, and certain to be out of hearing range, the women rolled in the cool soft sands of the Jamaican beach, laughing in hysterics, the slivered moon smiling down at their combined brilliance.

"You are a wonder, Mademoiselle Maggie Pye." Solange caught her breath a moment before falling into laughter again.

Maggie held out her hands, fingers splayed and heavy with the rings from the fop she had assisted to his feet.

"I could have been so successful without your assistance, Miss. But it would not have been near as much fun. Aye, you know I did not catch your name." Maggie shook her head at the discourtesy, something she was not known for. "Fah. Look at ye though. A woman what can drink me under and speak another language while at it. I think I will just call ye for what you must mostly be at this point, Blackstrap." Maggie wiggled her sparkling fingers.

Solange lost her focus for a moment. Blackstrap. She considered the name. "Oui. Blackstrap you may call me."

Maggie put a bejeweled hand out. "It is good to make your fine acquaintance, Mademoiselle Blackstrap."

"How long will you be on these islands, Maggie Pye?" Solange took the offered hand. "I should like to work with you again in the few days I will be here."

Chapter 5

Gennie leaned in to survey the maps again, noting with nostalgia the delicate hands never forced to hard labor though she sailed since birth.

"Forego more talk of where we have been and again onto where we are heading. Marrick tells me two days, maybe less. What say you, Maggie? Since we can say with certainty that the way will be clear."

She took another swig off the flask and swapped it with Maggie in exchange for the map.

"Aye, thanks in part, of course to Fair Ladies of the Sea and Winds." Maggie emptied the flask and handed it off to Marrick.

Upending the container offered nothing to his lips. Marrick scowled at the woman.

"I will want that back, sir, and full," Maggie grinned.

I will do my best lass, but remember, the seas have been quite quiet, thanks to the gods you so praise, and supplies are what they are."

Marrick bowed and turned away to find a barrel to drown himself in properly before bringing Maggie back her flask that he had had none of.

Gennie folded the map into her hand, crossed her arms on the rail, and leaned into the cool breezes. Two days to Topolis. Two days to fresh food, fresh water, and, with luck, fresh crewmen and fresher wenches. She pushed away from the rail.

"Aye," Marrick stopped at the sound of Gennie's voice. "Do any know if we have caught the other rat aboard ship?"

She turned enough to see Marrick shake his head.

"I have an ill feeling about this one," Gennie frowned. "It is not as careless as the others. It is waiting for something more than the next port."

"You do need more to drink, pretty," Maggie teased to hide that she, too, was concerned. "Paranoia is not becoming of lady nor captain."

Maggie tipped her head to return Marrick to the task of obtaining more rum. She hoped with the captain's mood the man would in fact return and not allow himself to distraction by drink or other folly as was typical. Still, Gennie knew how dangerous unaccounted for shipmates could be.

Gennie looked to Maggie for assurance. "I set the powder monkey to the task, captain. That little weasel knew all the best hiding places before we caught him up. He will find our rat. I have been looking with mine own eyes as well." Maggie was more than like the most qualified for the job of flushing out rats, and in sending the boy, young though he was at only ten years, Maggie knew well who best to partner with in the task. The little rodent, who had called *Ecstasy* home before any of her trusted crew, had grown much since his days sneaking between barrels and planks. Maggie had been the one to draw out and capture Sanji, and while he had bonded well into the family of the crew, he looked to Maggie and Gennie as one would a mother or nursemaid unwise to cross.

Chapter 6

Maggie stood at the prow of the xebec, eyes on the open water. Curiosity and fate might not wed for most, but in Maggie's case the pair coupled, and trouble never seemed to lead to anything less than good fortune and plenty of material gain.

"Miss Pye." Maggie lowered her spyglass at the sound of her name.

"Aye, captain," she addressed her current employer.

The old Greek stood not much taller than she, but his presence gave an air of enormity. His years were apparent in his grey-streaked beard, and he hid his bald head under an amber silk scarf and a broad-brimmed black hat. Maggie was fond of the man's style and sense of dress. She had grown somewhat fond of the man as an employer and ally as well, but it did not change her need to make use of his ship for her expertly charted course of action.

"I have come to trust your judgment in your short time as navigator, so I come to you on this recent development in our situation." The captain was quite often all flattery, but it was true in Maggie's case.

Maggie managed to shave days of travel from every jaunt the merchant ship had made since her hiring. By the close of the first month, she increased the xebec's courses by a third and, by that, the captain's profits.

"These waters, as I am sure you have heard, are plagued recently by pirates," the captain continued.

Maggie nodded, her face stoic in hopes not to betray her emotion.

"I should say, one pirate." The captain shook his head. "You are a woman who has seen much of the sea, so I know you understand such situations, but this is a bit different."

Maggie cocked her head and gauged the captain's expression.

"This ship is strange." He shook his head. "She is under the command of some sea witch with a bloody desire for any merchant vessel. There have been disturbing stories of her ability to cripple a ship from an incredible distance. But," the man scowled and he shook his head, "she never fires a cannon shot."

"It is nonsense, captain. Tall tales and rumor are a pirate's most powerful weapons," Maggie assured the man. "There are always survivors of the attacks?"

The captain gave a curt nod. "That is true. There are many slaughtered, but more are let free to limp to the nearest port. They are blessed in fact. She leaves not a chart behind, and, yet, the ships always find a way."

Maggie's eyes widened. "I know it," the captain continued. "It does not sound sensible to say a ship so ravaged is blessed, but any ship and crew that survives this monster at all is surely as blessed as any could be."

Maggie nodded but said nothing, her mind processing the story to find the truth between the lines.

"But, to the point of my revealing this news to you." The captain cleared his throat and clasped his hands behind his back. "Our current heading puts us in direct line with the last sighting of this demon. I trust you to find us a route equally efficient that will not take us into her jaws."

"Of course captain." Maggie beamed. "I am honored by your trust in my abilities."

"Very good then." The captain gave a short bow and turned away.

Maggie watched the man as he descended the staircase to the main deck. She turned again to the ocean when he had disappeared. She could not contain her pride, and as she raised her delicate gold spyglass to her eye a wide Puckish grin spread across her lips.

"Have faith in my abilities and the gods that guide me," Maggie voiced to the ocean.

"Captain." Gennie was becoming accustomed to the title.

Gazing at the tiny xebec in the distance, she acknowledged the sailor that had come up beside her, but only with a mumbled, "Aye."

"Langshe is ready." Gennie was grateful that at least a few of the crew could speak in languages she could comprehend.

None spoke a word of French, De Xavier had taught her a fair amount of Spanish, and her travels had given her a workable vocabulary in English as well as other European and Mediterranean tongues. The junk's crew, however, were as foreign as the ship itself. Chinese was a language that to Gennie's ears had first sounded more like madness, though she was fast catching on to more commanding words.

The crew had been more than happy to accept their new captain, after a fair amount of persuasion by the crew of *Despair*. The former captain had a more pitiful sense of direction than Gennie and gotten the vessel hung up on a reef that was well known to frequent, and even vigilant infrequent, ships sailing the area. Supplies depleted, morale was non-existent, and with the damage and body count caused by her run in with *Despair*, accepting Gennie's terms was more than a fair exchange.

"Just rock this one a little," Gennie trusted her instinct about this merchant ship. "I am certain there is something valuable on her."

The sailor, surprisingly close in height to the captain, hurried to relay the order after a curt nod.

Gennie worked to maintain a controlled pace as she made her way to the front of her ship. The first time she had ordered the dragons fired she had run like a child to watch. The display never bored her.

She listened intently as the unmistakable primary explosion rippled the water below. Hissing wildly, the langshe, as she understood to mean wave snake, burst from below the decks. It was never the projectile itself that Gennie saw since it was intensely too fast for any eye to witness, but the wake left a deep white-walled scar through the ocean.

Gennie flipped the spyglass to her eyes to follow the path to the langshe's prey.

Maggie was near the rail, admiring with awe the green-sailed ship just beyond the reach of the xebec's cannons, when the sparkling monster appeared in the water before them. A moment later an explosion tossed the merchant ship.

Sea spray, fire, and debris burst from the port of the xebec. It was not a direct hit to be sure, but if it was meant as a warning shot Maggie felt ill to think what damage could be done with proper aim.

Gennie could not contain her glee when the distant target nearly leapt from its position in the water from the wave created by the langshe's secondary and final eruptive burst. She spun away from the scene only a moment.

"To running!" Gennie bellowed at her crew. "Before our catch has a chance to think about the sting of that bite." Her lips formed a triangle. "Hoist a proper introduction!"

Ecstasy came to life, sailors bustling to ropes, handing out weapons, and rolling forth the cannons that might yet be used.

Gennie took her eyes from the imminent capture to look to the center and tallest of the five masts of the junk. Running up the rope to stop at the highest point of the mast, above the green of the battened sails, a black drape of fabric suddenly caught the wind.

Maggie followed the shadow of dark fabric as it ran up the center mast and caught the wind. Snapping in the breeze, and with the momentum of the ship, the design appeared in flashes.

The skull motif favored by pirates across the seas was most prominent flanked on either side by a trio of swords and below by a goblet. The design shone the same burning green as the sails.

"La fee verte," Maggie recalled the other drink her one time partner favored. "No," her mind working as she watched the ship approach cannon reach with supernatural speed. "Absinthian Skullerfly." Maggie took pride in her naming and prepared herself to meet the pirate captain.

Ecstasy overtook the fleeing xebec with the ease of a hare racing a tortoise. The assailing ship dragged along the side of the xebec. Planks slammed between the two vessels with practiced efficiency.

Maggie prepared alongside the rest of the merchant crew to fight for their lives and the cargo that meant their livelihood. Her readiness was as feigned as some others, though the reasons differed. If taken, Maggie knew that if asked, more than a few of the sailors aboard the xebec would shift alliance to save their own skin.

Gennie checked her appearance in one of the many unusual little mirrors that adorned the junk. She had gotten used to the twists and braids more typical of harem girls and dancers than pirates and sailors. She thought the look rather frightening for its unusual quality. The noise of the coins, beads, and bells at least gave notice to her entrance when she dropped on the decks of a captured vessel. She straightened the sleeves of her coat that did far less for her appearance, but she could not part with the old thing.

"Bonjour mes freres de mer." She always introduced herself first in French. "I am Blackstrap, Captain of Ecstasy."

Maggie approved of the juxtaposition the small pirate created. There was a spark of the once innocent, cunning, French sailor, now much more.

Gennie bowed. She took in the scene created by her nearly cannibalistic foreign crew. The devastating little demons enjoyed their work. It had disturbed her only the first time. Now it was a source of awe. They never killed more than half the defending crew, but the style and efficiency dispelled any thoughts that they would not enjoy killing more if need be.

Without severe alteration to her path, she stepped gracefully over decapitated and dismembered bodies, carefully avoiding deeper pools of blood and the occasional thick smears of brain or coils of entrails, making certain to keep somewhat clean her slipper-like shoes as she sought a new pair of boots.

Maggie was only moderately shaken by the severity of the attack. When she hid away, making herself look busy, below decks to gather and pocket what she could of the supplies, she had not expected to find such a level of slaughter, when she emerged.

"So, you are the sea witch so much talk has circulated about?" the xebec captain held a posture of pride Gennie had seen many times before. They all died with much less dignity.

"A witch," Gennie laughed, "is that now what they are calling me?" She scanned the crew. "Well then, maybe it should be that I not ask any here to join my crew. Rather, I should cast a spell to shift your loyalties or better still, turn the lot into gulls and fish?"

She waited for her words to be understood by some of her crew and listened to the snickering.

"You will join the sea in any case." Her tone shook some of the weaker members of the fallen ship.

"Then to the sea with us, witch." The captain leveled with Gennie.

She moved face to face with the man. Her height did not bother her when she was in the moments after a successful capture. Only after, when she was alone in her quarters while the crew congratulated one another in their own language and no one celebrated with her, did Gennie have her moments of uncertainty counting her luck thus far considering her situation, sex, and small stature.

"Not a man of my crew will reduce himself to be slave to a pirate or a woman," the man continued.

Gennie damned the Greek's pride.

"Aye," a woman's voice piped in. "Not a man, this may be true, but perhaps a woman."

Gennie and the xebec captain turned in unison to the direction of the voice. The junk crew allowed the woman through. A broad hat hid her face but not the gold and amber necklace around her pretty throat.

"Maggie Pye?" Gennie breathed the name with a smile growing on her lips.

She could not contain her joy at the sight of her former friend. Maggie removed her hat and dipped to a level reserved for deference to royalty into a well-practiced curtsy.

"Captain Blackstrap." It was the first time she had said the name aloud in many years, and the first time ever with the title before it, but it rolled off her tongue as beautifully as she hoped. "I am eager to be at your service as navigator, should you have need." She glanced up with a wicked grin for only a moment, "and more eager to replace for greater the one you now have if any."

Gennie gave in to emotion over appearances. She ran to embrace the woman. "Mademoiselle Maggie Pye, you have found your home!"

The women held for a long moment, but Maggie broke the moment with a level gaze at her friend that bespoke of keeping up appearances.

She returned her attention to the crews and the xebec captain. The glittering, cunning look that Maggie recalled from their first meeting took hold of Gennie's features.

"We have the only useful crew from this vessel." Gennie knew she had to redeem her girlish behavior. She released her crew with a nod. "The rest can join the sea as their captain ordered. Not as fishes though. Forgiveness, captain," Gennie shrugged, "I am no witch who can cast spells. Though in finding my old friend and bringing her to me in my time of most need, can I scratch your back as you have mine?"

Her wicked grin broadened as she watched as her translator, gathering her meaning, drew his blade behind xebec captain and plunged it deep into the man's back.

Gennie put an arm out to Maggie as the junk crew began the resurgence of the slaughter. Maggie walked past the woman and cat-stepped up to the body of the xebec captain. Thankful that the blade that felled the man did not slice the delicate fabric of his scarf. She pulled the silk from his bald head, and shook it out.

Removing her hat and setting it gingerly on the dead man's terror-frozen face, she said, "Hold this a moment, please, sir."

Gennie watched as Maggie tied the silk around her head and secured the knot. Maggie bent, retrieved her hat, then glancing a moment at the captain's hat that lay beside its owner's body, picked it up as well. She put her hat back on her head adjusting for just the right look and returned to Gennie's side.

Maggie set the black brimmed hat on the head of her friend and took Gennie's arm. She was fortunate that it was a size too large, else the twisted braids done by the dancing girls would not have fit.

"A captain should dress the part, pretty." Maggie looked

Gennie up and down.

"Are you to become my haberdasher and tailor as well then, Mademoiselle Pye?" Gennie raised her brow and side glanced at the woman as the pair made their way to the junk.

"Aye, pretty, navigation is my destiny and gods' chosen path, but I do dabble in other skills as well." Maggie tugged at one of Gennie's braids. "And you pretty, I see, enjoy the pastimes of the desert ladies."

Gennie pulled the braid from Maggie's hand, a falsely rueful look upon her face as she spoke. "This? Just something I do between voyages."

"There is always a good tale to drink to with you." Maggie teased.

Chapter 7

"Who stole it?" Gennie burst from her cabin, boots pounding a path down the corridor.

Sailors who had no idea the language Gennie spoke stumbled over one another to be clear of her warpath.

"A month!" Gennie raged, "a damned month I have had this junk on open water again and I have to deal with stowaways, thieves, rats?"

"Pretty," Maggie stepped into the corridor, "you are scaring the boys again. I know how much you are on your guard, pretty, but raging up and down the decks is no way to improve the crew's trust in you." Maggie tossed her flask to Blackstrap.

Blackstrap caught the elegant bottle. She drank the harsh liquid within.

"I must find this thief," she sighed. "It is not so much theft that bothers me. Supplies on this junk will not soon run short thanks to Ecstasy's ability to overtake lesser western vessels. It is just… if there are ways to access my cabin so readily." She sighed. "Maggie, we will be dead and gone before we can devise plan to do away with the mutinous lot."

Gennie halted her march. She opened and closed her fists at her sides as she worked to calm her emotions. She was too fast learning how correct De Xavier had been when he said she would need time to adjust to her new cage.

"Maggie," Gennie breathed and plastered a grin on her face, "our heading?"

"You are changing the subject, captain," Maggie shook a

finger, "but come on in, I will update you."

Gennie trusted very few of her new crew. Eternally indebted that Maggie's gods of fortune and the Mediterranean called the woman back home some years earlier, putting Maggie in a place to hear news of a strange ship with a rum guzzling female captain. Grateful too, to Maggie's curiosity and quest to find truth in the stories of this pirate woman taking entire fleets to the bottom with a curious and devastating weapon.

"I am in debt to your xebec captain for bringing you to me, Maggie," Gennie sighed and drank again. "The dancers trust me and are loyal for their rescue, but I can count on so few and understand so little of this language and crew. I need an ally to rally beside me in case of mutiny. Especially with that insane cook, Faye, aboard."

"There will be no mutiny, but we are heading deeper into the Asian seas." Maggie laid out the charts.

Gennie looked with curiosity and some concern. "Por quoi"

"You really do need my help," Maggie teased. "You are low on supplies, but have made such a name for this sea monster that no port will allow you anywhere near. And, you said yourself, you are out of dragons."

Gennie could not deny the truth of the woman's words. She had been quite proud the first few times entire ports had emptied or opened fire at the sight of *Ecstasy*, but the downside was clear after a stretch.

"Into the Asian sea, or past, and into ports where *Ecstasy* does not stand out so uniquely we will have much more luck," Maggie assured her.

"Fine and well, but in home waters it may embolden those that might turn against us," Gennie reasoned taking another drink.

Maggie knew how true this scenario was, but it was a better risk than the alternative.

"We will find and trap your rat before we reach your crew's home waters. He will serve a purpose, as an example, to repay for his trouble."

Maggie spent a fair amount of her formative years as a stowaway. Where Solange had the luxury of welcome aboard *Lenore* and openly, though with little choice, joined *Despair*, Maggie was forced to fend for her own needs and understood more about the lowest class of sea thief. There were rules, there were lessons, and as with any caste, there were types.

Maggie had met or been more than one in her youth. She crawled through the less welcoming portions of the junk. She recalled travels before meeting with navigators who trained her to be of use on a ship rather than an invisible nuisance.

"I will find you, my little rat," Maggie whispered into dark corners and alcoves. "I used to be you. Finding you is only a matter of finding who I once was."

It cost her several days and some of her captain's best chocolates, but Maggie had done as she knew she could and captured the stowaway before entering into Asian waters.

Gennie scowled at the vile creature. "What in the seven hells is that?" She pushed the blonde mop of hair out of the child's face.

"Yao nuu!" The boy howled as Maggie stilled him in a basket hold. She looked into honey-colored eyes that glittered and boiled with anger. The boy was soft-faced and bared a surprisingly good number of teeth. His hair, shoulder length and stick straight, was a complete mess.

Sailors gathered around entrance to the captain's quarters scattered as a tall, mousy-haired woman, an odd Gaulish find aboard a Far Eastern ship, marched toward them. The woman's apron was smeared with stains suspiciously like blood, and most of the men aboard shuddered to consider that it might be other than that of a small mammal.

"What is he yowling, Faye?" Gennie demanded of the cook that had been aboard the ship when commandeered and was a better translator than most.

The cook pushed through to the front of the crowd into the equally crowded captain's room. She looked wide-eyed at the sight of the child. "Aye, Captain, he. The boy calls you yao nuu."

The cook had little patience for anyone aboard the ship and, Gennie suspected, was more fierce with a knife than she let on. Gennie had not wanted to trust the woman after witnessing the violent way she removed sailors from the galley, but Faye spoke nearly perfect English as well as Chinese.

Gennie looked from the woman to the child to Maggie. "Bien. Mais what does that mean?"

The cook swallowed, smirked for a moment, but frowned again with a look from the captain. "Demon woman," she offered.

"Bizui! Fei-Fei duh Pi gu!" The boy spat at the feet of the cook. "Yao nuu!" He wailed at Gennie again.

Several native members to the crew crowing in the doorway snickered. A look from Gennie silenced them, but she smiled after a moment.

"And what did that mean?" Gennie laughed.

"He called me a baboon's ass," Faye frowned.

The cook, standing too close to the child's kicking legs, directly felt the full swing into her shin. The face made was worth another laugh from Gennie and a knife-wielding glare from Faye. The crew erupted in laughter and Faye turned her anger and knife to them.

Gennie put a hand out to stay the woman's anger before long pork could make a very real stay on the menu.

To the crew she ordered, "Back to work the lot of you! This ship does not sail herself!"

The crew, though only vague in the languages Gennie spoke, understood the tone well enough. Leaving Gennie, Maggie,

Faye and a handful of others, attention returned to the boy.

The rodent was full of venom, that much could be said. Tiny though he was, his being found and, subsequently, captured did not serve to put fear in his small soul. If anything, he seemed eager to fight himself to death if it came to that.

"Tell him to calm," Gennie commanded Faye.

As the woman tried to talk to the boy, Gennie tossed Maggie a length of rope and helped tether the wildling. After a moment more of watching the kicking, spitting, wailing scene, Gennie pulled from her pocket the remains of the brick of chocolate the boy had been caught stealing.

When searched, the child's possessions were not what one would expect a child his age to have at hand. Gennie glanced at the hook-like blade on the table beside her, the miniature crossbow, and the pile of explosives that had been in a pouch on the boy's hip. The short bow and clutch of arrows she found later when seeking out the treasures hidden by the child.

Gennie approached the detained creature with the chocolate brick. She knelt out of kicking range and watched.

"Yao Nuu!" the boy opened his mouth wide to pass the insult.

It was the move Gennie had been expecting and awaiting. She slammed a mouthful of bon bon into the open mouth.

The boy coughed. His eyes widened. He grinned, chewed the sweet, and swallowed. In complete defiance, he opened his mouth for another bite to be offered.

Gennie laughed. She sat back on her knees and shook her head at the child. "Ask what his name is while he is quiet," Gennie demanded.

Faye, backing away even as she questioned the child, spoke in the strange gibberish language that baffled Gennie.

"He is a half-wit." Faye crossed her arms in retort to the

boy's response.

"San-ji." The boy opened his mouth for another chocolate.

"Maybe he is no longer speaking the language of the ship?" Maggie offered.

Gennie sized up the child. The task of capturing him had not been easy. "Oui, he is much too clever and cunning to be a lack-wit."

Faye shook her head. "As you say, captain, but his speech is very poor for his age."

Gennie observed the shaggy golden locks on the boy. "Perhaps, but it is no more his native tongue than it is yours. He may know more than he is letting on."

"I am classically trained in the languages most used by the East India companies." Faye scowled. "This boy is no more than an animal."

This time Gennie broke another piece and gave him some, minding her fingers. She was enjoying the child's energy but would not press her luck.

"Sanji, oui," She mispronounced the name, "and I am Yao nuu, n'est pas?"

The conjuncture of languages confused the boy enough to make him think rather than wail. It also made Faye think again.

"The language is of the closed islands," she sighed. "San, means three, ji, or as he is pronouncing it, shi, is four. Or, it could just mean disaster." Faye smirked at the child.

Gennie stood and looked at Maggie and Faye. "So he does think, and learn, at least three-fourths as well as you." Gennie played with the name and numbers against Faye.

Faye glowered. "And, at least three-fourths your height, captain." She fired back.

Gennie ignored the jab, tossing it off with a grin.

The two women had been thinking the same thoughts since finding the boy. Neither desired to kill a child, even if it would drive home the point of Gennie's power better than the death of a grown, or even half-grown, man. Showing mercy might as well send a powerful message.

"We have all seen reformation of stowaways," Maggie noted.

"Do you still think our plan a good one then, Maggie?" Gennie looked at the boy.

"Tell him I will cut him free if he will work for this," she held out the chocolate, "rather than steal it. I think he will make a grand pirate."

Gennie and Maggie waited to gauge the boy's response. When he did not wail or kick again, Gennie grinned.

"Ask his age" She demanded.

"He says he is six years, captain," the cook offered.

Gennie took the knife from Faye and tossed it to Maggie. When she approached, the boy steeled his emotions. She recalled the last man Gennie had ordered a blade pulled on, decades older than this whelp, a captain, and all but pissing himself in preparation for his demise.

"You are brave or stupid, mignon enfant, but I know what it is to be small and what it is to be brave and stupid." Gennie knew the boy did not fully understand her, but he would learn.

Sanji did not run when the blades cut the ropes instead of his flesh. He sat a moment more before even making a move, then he opened his mouth and put out a hand.

Gennie and Maggie looked at one another. The women laughed, and Gennie tossed the last of the chocolate to the boy.

Chapter 8

Gennie grinned. The boy was as much or more a danger to stowaways than any grown man aboard the ship.

"I should have my wits," Gennie laughed at her own words. "Strange though it is for me to say, a drink might be the last thing I have need of."

"Carry on. Your captain shall be off to survey the goings on in less capable portions of the ship."

Gennie passed Marrick as she crossed the opening to the lower decks.

He held a full flask and bottle in his hands, a confused look upon his face. "Aye, I didn't take half the time I could've, poppet."

Gennie turned her head giving only her profile to the man. "But long enough for me to lose my thirst."

"What of your hunger then?" Marrick grinned.

Gennie's eyes narrowed. She understood the meaning but denied an answer.

"If you can't wait two days for entertainment send for me," he called after her.

The puckish smirk too familiar to the man appeared below the shadow of her hat.

"It may be there are others, more my taste, aboard this ship before you, on my list for entertainment."

Gennie sniffed, tossed her head and continued down the deck. Maggie laughed from her perch along the rail, just within earshot of the exchange. A dark look from the tall first mate worked to stifle her amusement, but only so far as to giggle. The captain would not have her morning rounds interrupted further, and Marrick was an easy fish to reel in at any time. Gennie adjusted her hat and coat. There were others far more entertaining. Her mind wandered as she made her way across the ironwood planks of the deck.

Blaze perched upon a sealed barrel, feet resting in front of him, his usual place toward the prow, with all of the deck in his sights and only the vacant ocean behind. Gennie watched from afar the smooth lines of the man's arms, his sinewy limbs honing the tools of his trade. She noted his tattoos, reapers both, on his upper arm and shoulder, visible only on the rare occasion the assassin was free of the weight of his leather tunic. The steel blades licked at the whet stone with every pass, clenched in long thin fingers. Before every landfall and after every kill, ritual, as any artist tends his gear while recounting the masterpiece completed. The mad assassin, swelled with satisfaction for his labor, to be certain. Gennie watched as his heel bounced in staccato rhythm as he sat. Here was a fine catch, a shark that bore waiting, watching, cunning, and preparation to net. Gennie toiled to strike upon the precise moment for years.

"Captain, ma'am, excuse." The voice shook Gennie from the spell.

"Aye, what is it?" She turned to see two young sailors, both female, struggling with a barrel.

She stepped aside to allow them passage. She eyed the pair for a moment and shook her head. What had possessed her to allow such hapless urchins to stay aboard, she wondered. She smiled, remembering how naive she had been when she had first commandeered a vessel, not much older than the two as far as she could guess, and of the two, at least one was an impressive thief, though always far too excitable in battle.

"Aye, now," Gennie scolded the passing girls, "don't be carrying more than you are able. I have no desire to have broken crew before we make land."

"It's not heavy, captain," Haitsu grinned. The girl had grown much since their first meeting. "Only a little more to make us stronger."

Chapter 9

Maggie and Blackstrap, as the gold-driven thief had taken to calling the rum-guzzling French girl, lay side by side watching stars pass over through an opening in the ceiling of the small grotto, listening to the tide against the walls of the stone caves of the beach, and reveling in the rewards of their latest caper.

Blackstrap stowed the jugs of rum under a pile of driftwood deeper in the cave. One bottle rested beside her head within easy reach. Maggie rolled onto her stomach and pulled an enormous ruby brooch from her bodice.

The woman admired the cut of the stone in the moonlight. Blackstrap curled on her side, hands under her head, to look. The items had come from one of the wealthiest estates on the islands. The pair decided their final escapade most profitable, though the risk had been much higher than others.

"Do you think we were followed?" Blackstrap yawned.

"No," Maggie sighed, eyes heavy as she gazed at the trinket. "I am sure they are still drinking the piss water rum you swapped with your haul. The wealthy are as lack-witted as their pockets are full."

"I was wealthy once," Blackstrap mumbled sleepily. "Am I lack-witted then?"

Maggie did not look away from her treasure, but she did make note to have that story retold to her. So many of the things Blackstrap said in their short friendship intrigued her. "No, pretty, when your pockets are empty your mind sharpens so as to fill them again."

Blackstrap smiled, her eyelids drooped. "Well, then Mademoiselle Maggie, you should be careful."

Maggie looked at her friend this time. "Why is that, pretty?"

Blackstrap giggled in half sleep. "Because your pockets have gotten so full you are stuffing your bodice. That could make you very dull indeed."

Maggie smiled at her friend. "You make a fair point." She stared at the brooch again and yawned. "I suppose in some ways then, it is good this is our last night together."

"Mmmhmm," was the only response Maggie barely heard before nodding off as Blackstrap had.

The shadowed figure watching by the entrance to the cave waited a moment more before inching closer to the sleeping thieves.

The young islander worked the estate. She witnessed the unfolding plot Maggie and Blackstrap so tediously performed. Though not fond of how her native people were treated by the settlers and sailors, still, she knew when the possibility for reward arose.

Maggie, dressed far above her station, in thread-of-gold-trimmed bodice and brocade overdress, parted with her favored hat to twist her hair in copper spirals. Blackstrap had been impressed at how much a lady the thief looked. She set Maggie's hat upon her head, however, and tipped it to hide her features. Maggie noted how well the hat suited her small friend. With dark coat and hat, she was not much more than a shadow. The women parted ways at the servant's entrance.

Within the walls, landowners and a few lord's and lady's wealthy associates gathered, gossiping, paying little mind to sobriety or propriety. Maggie slipped in among the daughters and young wives. Her intellect, however ill begotten, rivaled tutor-educated caged birds who were happier to twitter on about social nonsense than pressing issues of the real world. Maggie could play the part, could play any part, with a ready manner.

Blackstrap watched for only a few moments. Entertained though she was, she had business of her own to tend to. As Solange, she well could have fallen back into her society ways, but she was able, like Maggie, to take on the traits of a class she was not born.

In the kitchens, Blackstrap found cellar doors she set out to locate. Silently, she entered the cool darkness of the dusty room. After putting a line in the dust-caked glass, on each bottle, Blackstrap located her name.

"Must be mine then," the girl giggled.

In silence and speed, Blackstrap scurried, armful after armful, bottles to the cart at the top of the stairs. With each trip she also brought down bottles found near a seaside cave to replace the missing loot. The contents of these also rum though poorly aged and poorly made.

Her task complete, Blackstrap exited with laden cart and waited in darkness at the designated location for her accomplice. Though vigilant to avoid kitchens and corridors in use for the party, Blackstrap unknowingly picked up a follower, a short, round, dark skinned island native.

Questioned too often who her father was and what plantation he owned, Maggie, with loaded pockets, slipped off to the meeting place. She had gotten away clean, though, as practiced as she was.

The pair laughed all the way down to their temporary hideout thinking themselves out of sight and earshot. But at least one pair of eyes and ears had caught them and intended to take advantage of the skills of the two women.

Haitsu sidled along the walls of the cave, keeping both eyes on the women, making certain their eyes were not on her movements. The thieves, however, were sound asleep. Being at the peak of their guard during their plot, the late hour it had taken them to complete the task had made them weary. The young minds, thinking their location a secret and their plan so well-executed, slipped into comfortable dreams.

The island girl had also stolen from the household on several occasions. Her mother, a former woman of station on the island until the English arrived, passed on the secret entrances and ways of the house and land before her death. When the others had taken to the mountains, they used her information and her daughter to obtain supplies.

Haitsu put a hand over the glittering brooch. She listened to Maggie's steady breathing for a long moment. The girl closed her hand on the trinket and backed into the shadow.

Neither woman moved as Haitsu's large, dark eyes watched from the darkness.

Moving again, she made her way to the bottle above Blackstrap's sleeping head. Haitsu watched the young woman's steady breathing before she put her hand around the neck of the glass bottle. She watched intensely that she was still unnoticed before sliding the bottle in the sand.

The track was little more than a hand's breath in length when the young girl felt the hand on hers. She looked at Blackstrap, the woman's eyes remained closed though she gripped the bottle and Haitsu's hand.

Blackstrap pulled the bottle to her bringing the island girl's hand along with it. She hugged the bottle to her and curled tighter into a fetal position, effectively trapping Haitsu.

Haitsu swallowed as silently as she could, her eyes wide, anxiety welling as she wondered at the sort of person who snuggles a bottle of rum. The girl cursed in her mind.

She tugged gently, hoping at least to free her hand. There were plenty more bottles to be had, she knew, and she had planned to gather those after the two items nearest the women.

Haitsu, in clumsy, anxious rush to be free, twisted the bottle into Blackstrap's sleeping face. The woman woke with a curse.

"Zut alors!" Blackstrap sat upright, releasing Haitsu at last, and put a hand to her face.

The sudden outburst of her accomplice shook Maggie from her sleep enough to see the island intruder.

"Hey!" the woman rose fully awake from the realization that they were no longer alone.

Haitsu's eyes went wide. She snatched the bottle from the ground and rolled and kicked to her feet to dive for the opening of the cave at a run. Her bare feet pounding the sand, shoes dangling at her belt, she kept just ahead of the now trailing thieves.

"Thief!" both women shouted after the girl, looking at one another as they gathered the moment of humor in the situation.

Haitsu's breath running short, she made a last ditch effort to escape up a leaning palm. She was quick, despite stature, and practiced at shimmying up rough branchless trunk and into the pockets created at the top by dying branches.

Blackstrap, being equally small and quicker, though moderately drunk and very much unpracticed at shimmying up palm trees, made the trip barely her height before the girl descended at a greater speed sliding and slamming Blackstrap back to the sandy beach.

"Chien!" Blackstrap screamed at the girl.

Maggie caught up a moment later, but she made no move to try as Blackstrap had.

Blackstrap bellowed at the girl and reached for her pistol.

"Zut encore!" Blackstrap screeched.

Haitsu turned, secure in her escape, and waved the stolen

pistol for the women to see.

Blackstrap was nearly struck by the accidental shot fired, but the ball instead splintered the outer skin of the palm trunk. She was struck in the head by an assailing coconut instead. She stumbled back into Maggie with her hands on her head.

"Tu est morte!" the woman cursed at the girl.

Maggie snickered. Her friend turned on her.

"What?" Blackstrap's face was contorted into a foul appearance of frustration and anger.

Maggie laughed. Blackstrap put her hands on her hips.

"In the past several days and nights you and I, pretty, we owned these islands. I am certain there will be stories of our escapades and the items we managed off with." Maggie could stifle her laughter no more, "and yet, here we stand, the both of us, like fools, and you lucky she is a poor shot."

Blackstrap turned back to the tree and kicked the trunk, though her anger was evaporating.

"Pretty, we have been bested by a little girl." Maggie's laugh at last struck Blackstrap.

Looking up into the fronds then to the fizzy-haired girl standing dumb with a tiny ivory handled pistol in her hand, she strode toward. She sniffed back a laugh before breaking down as Maggie had. "I hate children."

"Hoy!" Maggie called after their laughter subsided some. "You there."

The women waited for a response or for the winded girl to sprint again. They received neither. Haitsu was listening and still struck by the noise of the weapon she had never once fired before in her life.

"Hoy! I say," Maggie repeated. Blackstrap waved her hands. "Come on now, sweetie."

"Sweetie is not my name." Haitsu aimed the pistol.

"Oui," Blackstrap called out, "then, s'il tu plait, petite, what is your name?"

"Like I am going to tell you!" Haitsu shouted to the women.

"Hey now, be polite to your elders," Maggie called back, the gap growing small between them.

Haitsu realized the situation then and how close Maggie was. There were two of them and they were closing the ground. She pulled the trigger again. Nothing.

Blackstrap dove to clear the last of the space and swiped the pistol from the girl as Maggie gripped her wrists.

"You have our word we will not harm you if you return Blackstrap's property, and mine as well," Maggie reasoned with the girl.

"Tell me your name, too, and I will tell you mine," Haitsu bargained with what little she had left.

"Maggie Pye," she offered.

"And Blackstrap Gennie." It was the first time she had said the name with her own tongue, and she enjoyed the sound.

"Haitsu Momo Tamu." She twisted her head to look at each woman.

Looking at the women closer and in the growing light, she found humor in their names. Named after the bird so fond of shiny objects was the one that had stolen the large ruby, and many other pieces of expensive jewelry from the guests at the party. The other, the one so attached to the bottle, which Haitsu knew read Blackstrap, was named after the rum.

Blackstrap and Maggie looked at one another after the girl had said her name. Blackstrap stepped away.

Maggie waited until Blackstrap demonstrated how to reload the emptied pistol before releasing the girl. Haitsu paused just out of reach to again gauge the motives of the pair.

Simultaneously, Maggie and Blackstrap put out a hand for

their treasures.

"You are a good thief, little one." Maggie caught the brooch as it was tossed to her.

"I am curious if the petite fille knows just how good." Blackstrap caught the rum bottle, eyes wide, and coddled the glass to her chest.

Haitsu still readied feet to the ground for fear the women would give chase again.

"You are the thieves the entire island is talking about." Haitsu did not believe the words as they came from her lips.

"None other." Maggie curtsied.

Blackstrap shrugged with her wicked grin still on her face.

"So, young one, you are what," Maggie sized up their young opponent, "near a decade our junior? Keep up such behavior," the woman shook a finger, "and you will be more of the devil than either of us."

Haitsu was confused by the statement. "Are you telling me to change my ways?"

"Mais non, of course not." Blackstrap took a long drink off the bottle. "We are leaving today. It is good to know we do not leave the island to be bored by our absence."

The pair linked arms then and promenaded down the beach back the way they had run. Haitsu watched for a long moment before following.

"Wait!" She looked at Maggie's back then to Blackstrap's.

The women waited to hear the girl's words. She made her way to block their path.

"Do you need help with your other treasures?" Haitsu smiled. "For a small fee I will help you carry your things wherever need be."

Maggie and Blackstrap looked at one another then at the small girl and her offer.

"For a small fee." Maggie stated as per the nonverbal agreement she had made with Blackstrap.

"These are really very heavy," Haitsu groaned as she heaved along, back flattened with the weight of the sacks of rum and trinkets.

"You will be stronger for your trying to carry just a bit more than you can handle," Maggie noted.

She and Blackstrap, arms linked, lead the way empty handed as the girl carried all of their belongings.

"You know, pretty, after today there is a part of me that thinks having a child or two might be quite useful," Maggie tittered.

"Aye," Haitsu groaned again but continued to trudge along.

Gennie and Maggie laughed again, but moved to take some of the load off the young girl.

"Don't worry Haitsu, on a ship everyone pulls their own weight." Gennie smiled at the girl. "Especially in times of trouble."

Maggie nodded in agreement. "And there is a fair share of trouble always around Blackstrap."

J. J. M. Czep

Chapter 10

Gennie smiled at her young crew as they continued on their way. She returned her gaze to the barrel at the prow. Blaze was gone.

"Your focus is waning." Gennie felt the blade on her throat before the words had left the air.

"You will be sure, I trust, to always keep me on my toes." She leaned back into the man and away from the blade. "One of these days, though, the crew will think you are truly out to have my head."

"And I will off them, too. They can wait their turn," Blaze hissed into her ear.

"We make land in two days. I want you to stay aboard ship this time." Gennie pushed the blade aside with her fingertips.

"Finally, some peace," Blaze coughed.

"I knew you would approve."

"Your trust confuses me," Blaze slid the dagger between a fold of cloth and tucked the weapon into a pocket in his boot.

"You carry more blades than I would care to offend, sir, but, I know you prefer guns, one in particular that I carry. You will not allow harm to come to my vessel, my crew, or my person while that is so." Gennie locked her gaze with the blue eyes of the assassin.

"True." His eyes burned the word into her soul.

"There may be trouble though." She changed the subject so

as not to fall into the piercing orbs.

Gennie tried to remain calm though she knew the assassin could smell fear, no matter if he were the cause or no.

"A little action will keep me from getting too bored." He walked back to the barrel he perched on prior.

"I fear it may be more than just a bit of action. Possible more than even you can handle. Fire a warning at the first sign of danger."

"Fire and change remind me. Cooler weather is finally coming," he noted and pulled a black shirt from the deck and over his head before walking away.

She hated when he turned to small talk and sarcasm, a means of keeping what he really wanted to say. Gennie, though, also spoke of things other than what was on her mind at the sight of the assassin. She watched the sinewy muscles of the man as he walked away, a feline-like air to the movement. She knew he watched though his gaze faced away from her. He always watched, everyone, but most especially the captain that had once been merely a young woman with fortune and infuriating persistence to corner him.

Chapter 11

The young man smiled down at the strange French girl found unescorted, waiting at his gondola's slip, dressed in clothes more rightly suited for a young fisherman or sailor than a lady. She spoke like a lady though, and had money to pay him twice due for a tour of the more secret places of the city.

"I hear Venice is tres belle, cette printemps," Solange flirted with the boatman.

"Masquerade season brings many beautiful sights, signorina."

Solange sat up from her pillows. "Masquerade? Tu sais." A dreamy expression crossed the woman's face. "I have always wanted to attend a masquerade ball."

"Si, there are several every evening, my lady," the youth smiled, "but proper attire is required."

Solange narrowed her gaze. "Well, I would imagine so. Mais, I understand your thinking."

She tossed a pillow at the boatman, he ducked, projectile flopping into the river behind and slipping away.

"Take me to the nearest and best costumer in this city. And he best be quick with his needle or I will be quicker with mine." Solange leaned back into the remaining pillows.

With minimal persuasion, verbal, physical, and financial, the dressmaker did prove to be very quick with his work. It did help that Solange, being a common size, was able to fit into a dress, meant for another with a less pressing time constraint. It was not her favored color, but pink did suit Solange well enough. The pearl trim of the bodice complimented Solange's sea-bronzed skin. Skirts, like fresh fluffed meringue, by fortune of volume hid the trouble of her inability to successfully obtain more formal footwear.

As she stepped into the boat with the gondolier's aid, he noted with crooked brow the weathered boot glimpsed beneath clouds of ruffle. The boot was, however, the only giveaway that this was the same passenger he had delivered and promised to wait for.

"It is as I guessed." The youth kissed Solange's fingertips. "You are indeed a noble lady. My curiosity lusts for your story."

Solange smiled. "I am sure it is my story you lust for, and that of any other lady."

She settled her skirts with care and leaned into the pillows as before. Her appearance betrayed nothing of the sea-maid that had earlier behaved and spoken so crudely.

"So, mon consort, I have need to find un fete to suit this costume, non?" Solange pulled a white lace fan from her matching purse. "Take me to the best masquerade in all of Venice!"

"I am sorry, senorigna, that is a request I cannot grant." The boatman laughed. "Money and force will not gain you invitation to the Count's Homage of the Lily. No one but the most trusted friends are allowed near the front entrance, and you have no mask. I will take you to one of the town fountain dances. They are equally amusing, I am sure."

"And I am sure they are not." Solange had one night in Venice. The ship would leave without her, she was certain, if she did not make her way to port before the next night. "I am certain, though, mon amour, that you are acutely aware of less obvious entrance to the count's estates." Solange slowly opened the fan to its full span and lowered it, until the lace caressed the row of pearls, at her breast.

Though the boatman was not the most fluent in the language ladies spoke with their fans, he could not miss the meaning of the gaze above the gesture.

"I know of one way." He smiled, "but it will cost."

A dark shadow sidled along narrow walkways surrounding the canals, used to maintain the routes or rescue capsized vessels. Rescue was not in the mind of this traveler, though, quite the opposite. Blaze held his position as a solitary gondola skirted past, silent ripples left in its wake. He thought it odd, a guest taking the back entrance to the mansion, but did not allow the diversion to stray his duties. He pulled the smiling black-jeweled Venetian mask from his head. Blue eyes flashed through the sockets of the false face. He smoothed his black hair back into place and dusted wrinkles carefully from his long coat, a glint of metal revealing as he straightened his long arms.

The boatman slowed the gondola to a practiced and faultlessly silent stop in the secret slip at the back of the count's home.

"The count uses this as entrance for the red ladies and courtesans he entertains frequently."

Solange let a sly look cross her face. "And how is it that this humble gondolier knows of such private liaisons?"

"If you will not tell me your story, lady, you will be denied the telling of mine." The boatman offered a hand to guide his passenger to solid ground.

"I will not be baited. There are stories greater than yours boatman, they await within these walls. My story did not become what it is or will be by passing greater things for small."

Solange bowed, waved her fan, pivoted, and sashayed into the secret tunnel leaving the young boatman wanting everything from a woman he knew nothing of.

The light ahead set Solange at ease. The boatman had not steered her into a trap that would end in his getting more than she yet offered any man. She stopped and turned a moment at a sound in the narrow tunnel. Her mind moved that it would be wiser to keep moving rather than risk a fight.

The boatman had given more than entrance to the masquerade through his knowledge. The tunnel opened to a corridor of apartments, all silent, but full of all a courtesan to a count could desire, or a count could desire of his courtesan. A mask, a few fine glittering objects made their way into Solange's possession. She made her way room to room. Satisfied, she closed her wrist pouch, adjusted the trinkets matched to her attire, and pulled the alabaster glass and pearl beaded mask down, replacing her deviant grin with demure soulless moon face. Following sounds and servants, the ballroom bloomed into Solange's vision. The captain would not believe it if she described it to him, which of course she would not, but to Marrick she might.

Blaze followed the courtesan in pink and white. She would lead him directly to his target, he was certain no one would be closer and more privately associated with the count than one of his paramours. She seemed younger and less demure of step than most of her kind. If she was new to the trade that would make the count even more focused.

Solange moved across the floor from partner to partner for hours. What most fascinated her, she found, was the man with a black skull mask and leather coat. He watched her from her first sight of him and seemed unduly interested in whom she turned to partner. He never danced any of the dances, but continued to move deftly elsewhere before drawn into the rotation. No other guest appeared to take much heed, but Solange, vigilant from prior exploits and ever open to danger, watched.

"Monsieur, I notice you do not dance." Solange had secreted her way beside the man in black, but had failed to startle

78

him with her sudden appearance at his side.

"I notice you dance with all the guests equally without much attention to your duty to your master," the man answered.

"I am sorry?" Solange was confused by the statement and the man's demeanor.

Blaze's blue eyes glanced down at the girl from behind his mask, making them all the more stunning. Solange was dazzled.

"You are not a guest here any more than I." Solange took surprise in her honesty.

The effect was as desired, however. The man in black looked at her straight on with those glinting gems.

"Who are you?" She was faster than he with the question. Solange had the upper hand, but could not break the spell his eyes cast.

Blaze grabbed the girl's wrist. He pulled her into the alcove behind them, startling an amorous young couple masks askew. Blaze had the pair moved out and scurrying with a glare from the eyes that so mesmerized Solange.

"I could ask the same thing," he hissed at the girl.

"But you did not," Solange hissed in return.

Blaze frowned at Solange and released her arm. Solange rubbed her wrist. She sized her opposition and the situation. He was well armed, she realized, with distance and time no longer an interference.

"You are not here on benevolent orders, monsieur." Solange stepped closer.

Blaze expected the girl to run and give warning at discovery of his motives. Her almost amorous advance was unexpected. He met many in his occupation, and this courtesan was not behaving as her counterparts. "I'm here on paid orders, but I'll practice my craft on you first, lady."

Blaze pushed his coat aside to reveal a row of blades

Solange had glimpsed prior, though not fully.

"Oui, so you are an assassin," Solange grinned, "I have found the more exciting story than the boatman's."

Solange put a hand on the man's chest. "The count. I know which one he is. He recognized my face," she tapped the mask, "though he does not know me. I can get him alone, if you promise me something for my part in this."

"I can do my job without help," Blaze protested and moved to leave this mad young woman.

Solange held Blaze by the barrel of his own pistol, a small, ivory handled single shot. It was a lady's gun by creation, but it served the assassin well for its discretion. The gold barrel reflected in his blue eyes.

"Your name, monsieur, will allow you passage. Your cooperation will allow you completion of your orders."

"Blaze." He glared at the small nuisance. "Now, my gun, please." He held out an open palm.

"Sol." She offered only half of her name and the gun not at all. "You have another, and the knives will do the job well and with more silence."

Blaze was more than annoyed with this deviant pickpocket wench. He did not ask, though he wondered viciously, how she knew of his other weapons and wondered what other information this Sol, had taken without his offering.

Solange did as promised. Tucking the assassin's pistol away with other souvenirs of the evening, she made her way through the crowd to partner with the count. She turned the target with a flick of her fan across her face and a gaze away from the ballroom and into the hallway where she originally entered.

Willingly the count trailed this favored courtesan, or so he thought. Solange glanced back at the count. Beyond his shoulder she locked eyes with Blaze and dropped her fan to her side.

"Of course we are friends, my dear one. I should hope we are so much more by now." The count caught Solange by the waist. His thick fingers tugged at the lacing of her bodice, his breath, a blend of soured wine, cheeses and meats turned Solange's stomach and expression making her glad for the ever-pursed lips of the mask.

She did not suffer the undesirable advances long. Blaze turned the count's chin in his hands and pulled his finest blade the width of the man's throat. Solange sidestepped a space to avoid spoiling her gown with the count's blood.

In Blaze, Solange had found something new. Her eyes shone. She stared at the assassin from the other side of the fallen count.

"You will ruin your slippers." Blaze tossed his mask into an unoccupied room, and smoothed his hair in single motion. He cleaned the blood from his blade and returned it to an empty pocket in his coat beside several others.

Solange broke her gaze to look where he gestured. The steadily growing pool of blood crept to her skirt. She lifted the hem.

Blaze looked at the worn boots revealed as Solange stepped away and around the count.

"That's not typical footwear for a courtesan."

Solange dropped her skirt. "I am no courtesan. I am a sailor, aboard *Lenore*," she stated.

"Don't care." Blaze took a step toward Solange. "My gun." He held his hand open to receive the item.

Solange shook her head. "Non, monsieur."

"You have no use for it. Return my gun." He advanced on her, his eyes flitted up and down the walk.

Solange drew the gun level with the much taller man's chest. Blaze paused.

"Don't think I won't shoot," Solange threatened, she

waivered only slightly. "I want to know more about what you do. I want to know why you killed this man."

"What?" Blaze was not pleased about this turn of events. If he did not vacate soon the search would be on for the count, and he did not care to end his career because of a delay by some princess in boots. "Fine. Fine, I'll tell you, but not here."

Solange followed willingly, her feet taking two steps for each of Blaze's. He would take her back to his temporary home. There he would again have the upper hand. He would take the gun and maybe allow the brat to return to her ship unharmed.

Solange follow Blaze, she did not know where, but the man would lower his guard in a location of his choosing. She could learn more about the pistol then, possibly, more about the man.

The boatman waited for Solange to return. His face fell at the sight of Blaze at the girl's side, both tossing glances over shoulder.

"I thank you for waiting, my friend." Solange stepped into the boat with no aid from the boatman.

"Halt." Blaze glared at the boatman's block. "I have not heard the lady ask for your company."

"You're a fool." Blaze shoved the man aside and dropped into the boat. He would not sit in the pillows, but instead stood and watched the shore and Solange alternately.

"Take the first right." Blaze ordered the gondolier.

The gondolier followed the confusing turn-by-turn directions of the man without argument, though he could not say why.

Blaze did not bark the orders. He only said where to go in a smooth level tone. He had never been disobeyed, except by this girl. He glared at the content Solange draped among the pillows.

"My jobs are well organized, executed one step at a time, flawless," Blaze stated and gave the order for the boatman to slow. "You're outside of that plan."

"You should not be so structured. Not everything plays by the book," Solange offered.

"You shouldn't tell people how to do their jobs," Blaze grumbled sarcastically.

"I have until daybreak," Solange said. "I will return your weapon to you, if you teach me how to use it."

"Impossible." Blaze glared. "I am not a master here to train you. Give my gun back, It's my best one."

"Stop." Blaze ordered the gondolier.

The gondola slid into place. This was a major stop in daylight hours. Other gondolas, empty, swayed and bumped and softly splashed in the darkness, heard though barely seen.

With the grace and knowing of a feline, Blaze stepped from the vessel. He did not wait to assist Solange from her seat. The girl struggled in her skirts and pillows before the gondolier helped her to her feet and onto shore.

"You should not go with him, lady," the boatman pleaded.

Solange looked from the boatman's face to his hand so roughly wrapped around her arm. "I thank you for all you have done for me, monsieur, but it is time we part ways."

Solange leaned and kissed the boy on the cheek, far less than her typical farewell kiss. In view of this assassin she did not want to offer more. He captivated her. "Adieu." Solange waved, but the gondolier made no sound or move in farewell as he pushed his boat into the ink.

She allowed herself to be caught up in the grasp of the assassin as she watched the boatman slip away. The blade at her collarbone was cold from the night air.

"I'm going to ask once more, nicely, for my gun back; then I'm going to take it," the assassin hissed.

"Why not take it by force now and save the trouble?" Solange leaned into the man and away from the cool metal.

"I don't like to leave unnecessary messes behind," he whispered, "and, I'm not getting paid to."

"Though happily you would do so if the money were right?" Solange put her hand between the blade and her throat.

Blaze could not believe his hand hesitated. Payment or no, he would kill to protect his tools. This woman had his favored pistol for more time than he allowed his victims to see it, and still she was breathing, and he was breathing her. Lost in thoughts not typical to his cool demeanor, he failed to notice the girl turned to face him without increasing her distance.

"Let me keep it a small while, a souvenir of our meeting." Solange smiled up into the blue eyes of the assassin.

She was trying so hard not to lose her concentration. She locked eyes a moment more before pressing her lips to his. The assassin shoved away at the advance. He placed a foot on the hems of her skirt and Solange splayed onto the cobbled street. The casualty was unintentional.

"Sorry." The apology no more than a whisper and not something he typically did.

Marrick rounded the corner to see Blaze standing over Solange. He drew his sword, one he carried only when he felt there would be a need. The near seven-foot claymore drew a line of sparks where the tip scraped the stones before Marrick swung the blade high over his head.

The assassin, quicker by a good stretch, sidestepped the attack without thought.

"Quick little rat aren't you," Marrick cursed.

"Quick enough not to waste time with the likes of you," Blaze called as he leapt onto a wall and seemed to walk up the building to be out of Marrick's reach.

Marrick shot a glare at Solange before giving chase to the assassin.

"Marrick don't!" Solange called after the man.

Marrick refused to hear the girl call out to him, but instead ducked the points of the knives thrown by the assassin.

"You're not worth the cost of my weaponry, fop," Blaze cursed. "Let the wench have the gun. I'll kill for another, and you won't always be at her side when I come for what is mine."

"I don't know what you're goin' on about, boy, but I'll have your head on a spit. Come down here and fight like a man," Marrick cursed.

"Marrick." Solange's legs could scarce keep apace with the long legs of either man. "Let him go, for now. I will know how to find him when I need him." She held the gun aloft. "Assassin. I will have your allegiance some day, I swear on this."

Blaze shook his head at the bold young woman. "If I didn't think it would cost me my career and my life I would have you and my pistol."

Blaze dropped into the shadow of an awning. Only after landing did he realize the meaning in the misspoken words. Solange returned the pistol to its place in her purse before making eye contact with Marrick.

"What was that about?" He barked at her as he advanced.

He grabbed Solange, proceeded to toss her over his shoulder, and marched in the direction of the ship.

"You are hurting me," Solange complained.

When they were at a distance Marrick felt was clear of any new attack from the assassin he released Solange, dropping her roughly, and continued to walk at his brisk pace.

"Over a gun," he grumbled. "Over a pretty little gun, you'd've been killed."

"It was not about the gun," Solange sighed. "It was about the man."

Marrick stopped so short, Solange, eyes still gazing at the awnings, collided with him. Marrick was glaring down at her, the look of a jealous lover sparking in his eyes for a moment before Solange's soft, confused gaze brought the platonic concern to the light again.

"What could you see in a cur like that," Marrick growled. "He'd've killed you if I hadn't been there to rescue you. Again."

"Rescue." Solange had flinched at the jealous look in her friend's eye, but she ignored it with the sting of the insult. "You had no call to rescue me. I am learning quite well how to care for my own troubles here and there," Solange assured him as she swaggered past and into view of the slips.

"I don't believe your arrogance," Marrick groaned. "A way with a sword wasn't the only trait you adopted from me."

Solange made her way to the plank of *Lenore*. The captain waited at the top of the way. Typically, his posture and presence upon her returns caused Solange to cower and make for her hammock. Tonight though, she had been through too much. She did not allow the captain so much as a word before pointing a quieting finger to her lips and moving past.

"Lovely dress." The captain shook off his awe at the girl's behavior after setting an eye on Marrick.

"One of these days you are not going to bring her back," the captain said.

"No," Marrick leveled with the man, "Oh, no, I'll always bring her back." He paused to lock eyes with Solange before she disappeared below the deck. "Kickin' and screamin' if I have to."

Solange pulled the gun from her purse. She had stashed the gown and other trinkets in her trunk. As she lay on her hammock she aimed the tiny gun at the ceiling above. "Bang." She dreamt of the man she would have working for her, training her someday when the word pirate could be used to describe her person truly.

Chapter 12

Still, there was the issue of the other stowaway.

Gennie did not like the idea of Sanji hunting the wretch alone. Attribute it to woman's intuition. She knew the little rat had claws, but some things even he could not flush out.

Her mind was still plagued by visions in the night, but too much else filled her thoughts in the daylight. The ship needed tending and plans needed made before the next port.

As much as Gennie knew the stories of her crew and trusted them because of that, knowledge the assassin knew only passed whisper to whisper on the ship. All would learn in time who they really were, beyond legends that might spread by their lips or the lips of others.

The ship had a story, too. One that few would believe upon the sight of her and fewer still after time spent understanding the ship and her captain.

Ecstasy was Gennie's near to five years, before that the opium trade junk *Mei Hei Feng*. It was not a marvel that Gennie treasured her ship. Equally, they shared a mottled history that took them through adventures few would have endured with such fair ends.

The stories the boards and cannons could tell would take a lifetime, and more stories stretched before her. Gennie studied the lines on the back of her hand as she followed them from the grain of the wood rail she rested on. There would be time to add many more lines. Another ten years, another five, or maybe less, a pirate does not have a set date of retirement. Gennie liked it that way. Never knowing what might rise with the next horizon was all part of the adventure.

Topolis was close to the place she obtained *Ecstasy*. The nostalgic irony of fitting the last piece of her crew into place near where it all began was not lost on Gennie. The threat of others she might meet with was not forgotten either. Solange attracted as many enemies as friends. Some she was not certain the camp they would be in upon next meeting. She collected names from the acquaintances as well. In some respects, it was useful. She had not begun looking to create a reputation, though each name took on a legacy all its own.

Chapter 13

The captain's footfalls rattled the steps to where Gennie stood, head bent over rolls of charts, maps, and notes. She did not raise her eyes.

The door banged against the wall. De Xavier held it back with his right hand, his sword hand. Gennie knew he was trying not to put that hand on his weapon.

"Where are we?" His voice projected but remained controlled even in his anger. Ever charming even when about to explode, it seemed a side that only Gennie could draw forth.

Gennie's gaze wandered from the desk to level with the captain's glare. She looked lazily around the cabin and back at the man in the doorway.

"In the archives," Gennie offered.

He swept into the room and jabbed a finger into the middle of one of the maps. "No, Cinta," he hissed out the name. "Where," stabbing at the map, "are we?"

Gennie rested her palms on the edges of the desk. She leaned over the table and cocked a shoulder toward the captain as she looked from the point of his finger denting the map into the smoldering brown eyes.

"The ocean," she grinned.

That did the trick. The captain swept his hand and the papers beneath it off the desk. "You are the worst navigator I have ever had the misfortune to know, no less have on my ship!" He bellowed and rounded the table toward Gennie. "We are lost!

Again!"

Gennie stood her ground. The captain never took a hand to her, or any of his crew. He left that to more sadistic crewmen. She allowed the man to close the distance and stare down at her, temper leveling once more. She snapped a paper out and held it beside her face, her free hand pointing to a location near the base of the map.

"Here," she assured the captain. "I am never lost, as you are never wrong. We are merely exploring the unintended. I have yet to know your full excuse."

With both hands, he snatched the unusual map. "This map is not any language and not any place I have seen." He flicked the paper with the back of his hand and looked for Gennie's response.

"Because it is not of any language or place you have been, captain." Gennie slid over to peer around his shoulder at the map.

She pointed again to their location then traced a path down, across, and off the western point. "We came this way, off the tip of Africa. We must have caught some current that pulled us here."

"How do I know you did not draw this map, yourself?" the captain asked over his shoulder.

Gennie shrugged, "Because I do not know how to write in this language, which I think is Arabic, or maybe Hebrew." She tilted her head right, then left.

The captain stepped back and shook the map at the girl's face. "What?" He shook his head. "How do you know this foolishness?"

"Languages, captain?" Gennie tilted her head, a half grin on her face. "You are going to ask how I know a language? Vraiment?" The captain's mood was ebbing. This captive–turned-temporary-navigator was incompetent with most map work, but she knew how to navigate his moods. "But, I cannot read this, only recognize. My guess, we are in the Indian Ocean. Possibly near Indonesia."

"When you do learn to read it, let me know how to get back out of the Indian Ocean. Possibly away from Indonesia." He rolled the map and handed it off to Gennie. "This is not making my captaincy look very promising."

She took the scroll. She was not so foolish as to think he was not serious. As soon as she heard the door latch she dove for the shelves of books. She had no idea what to look for, but she had to find it quickly.

Upon taking *Despair* under his command and marooning the former captain, De Xavier made quite clear what he expected of his crew, especially the newest and least trusted.

*   *   *

A thundering shudder rocked Gennie from her perch on the table. The next buried her under books, maps, and scrolls.

The door flew open as Gennie pushed a heavy stack off her legs.

"Captain wants all hands on deck. Now!" The blonde woman in the doorway was a beauty as well as built to stand up to more abuse than Gennie. Talena, the first mate, bellowed orders, but Gennie knew other sides to her. "Are you sure you are okay?"

Gennie nodded, rubbing the back of her head. "What was that?"

Talena lifted Gennie from the floor with ease of a child picking up a doll. She did not wait for her to follow once she was on her feet though.

"You will see." Talena took the steps two at a time.

Gennie followed, curiosity overcoming the throbbing pain in her skull.

The captain barked orders from the helm. Talena ran to her duty to send others to theirs.

Gennie stepped onto deck, the full power of the galleon *Despair* swept into position. Gennie had not seen this much of the ship's fire power since it inflicted it on *Lenore*. Then she had been on the wrong side and not fully appreciated the beauty of the dance. She was awestruck.

The eight-hundred-ton goddess of the sea was a prime example of Spanish engineering. Masts, like spires stabbed the sky and billowing ink-black sails, rippled in the sea air. Gennie watched as a pair of sailors hoisted the jack, which was emblazoned with crossed bones behind a skull, a map clenched in boney jaws, and flanked on the left with a blade and on the right with a goblet. The first time Gennie had seen the flag she had not thought about the symbolism. A white skull meant pirates, always. She was drawn to the image now that she understood it.

Gennie sidestepped as a pair of silver-banded eights were rolled into place. She counted the cannons, at least seventy on the main and split decks, but she knew there were more below. This was only the one side of the ship. Like fiery eyes, a twin pair of five-pound cannons mounted to swivels. In a farewell or to slow pursuit, a half dozen more eights lined the rear rail. Though she lacked speed, *Despair* was not a ship easily matched in size and power.

Gennie felt more than a little lost as to what to do. She had not been allowed often above decks, and then it was only for short spans of time. She had become navigator following the mutiny because of her ability to read, not her ability to read maps, this imprisoned her in the ship's archive and map room much of the time.

"Cinta!" Gennie turned her head toward the sound.

The captain beckoned her to his side, at the helm. Grateful to have purpose, she hurried to his side. He handed her the eyepiece. Gennie put the device to her eye and worked the focus.

She allowed the captain to direct her gaze.

"There," he stopped her.

In the half-light of morning, the shape was difficult to make out. It was a ship, that much was easy enough, but unlike any either had ever seen.

"I know you have traveled to and seen some very strange things," the captain spoke into Gennie's ear, "but, tell me, Cinta, have you ever seen such a ship?"

Gennie worked the focus on the eyepiece. "No," she sighed, "never, captain."

De Xavier took the scope gently from her hands. Gennie watched the man watching the distant ship. "How far do you think that is?"

Gennie looked with naked eyes. She could easily make out the ship, though it looked more a sloop than a full-size ship. "I would not know. Too far yet to fire upon?"

The captain nodded but did not look away from the strange ship.

Gennie paused as she realized. "It fired on us?" De Xavier locked eyes with Gennie. For the first time she saw fear in the man's eyes.

"At that distance?" Gennie pointed. "De Xavier, it is not possible!"

"Not enough to cause severe damage, true." He walked and bid her follow. "What disturbs me more is where the attack struck."

Gennie followed the captain down the steps to the main deck.

"Talena," De Xavier bellowed to the girl. "You have the deck. Prepare for anything!"

Talena saluted, but glared a moment at Gennie.

The pair continued down the decks, down, down, to the bilge ladder. De Xavier held out a hand. "Ladies first."

Gennie stared down the opening for a moment, gathering scattered thoughts, still struggling to make sense of their descent. She felt for the steps, one foot at a time, De Xavier aiding her until she could put a hand on the rungs. He followed when she called all clear. The water was waist high and Gennie was glad to be wearing cotton breeches and dark colors. Over her shoulder she watched De Xavier remove his coat and sword belt, draping the items over his shoulder before descending fully into the water.

"Where are we going?" Gennie pressed.

"There." The captain directed Gennie's attention to a glowing section a few feet away, a cluster of carpenters repairing damages.

Gennie approached. The wall looked as if a battering ram had struck it, though with just enough force to split a few boards.

"I cannot imagine it at a closer range," De Xavier whispered.

"The water was deeper before, captain. We have it under control, though we will need to make for land soon if the repairs are going to be made to hold." One of the carpenters shook his head. "What weapon does this?"

"Captain." Gennie put a hand on the man's arm. "De Xavier." She shook gently.

He looked down at her. This time fear was omnipresent.

"De Xavier. I do not mean to be contrary, but you are certain this damage was inflicted by that ship, and not a reef we did not notice?"

"It was not a reef, Cinta." De Xavier stared at her. "A reef drags. Shallow or deep, its mark leaves a long scar, not an impact like a cannonball."

"I knew you had thought of that. I did." Gennie was trying to calm the man. "But think, captain, this weapon. As deadly as it is, used against us, how deadly would it be to your adversaries? No other would have such a thing or defense against it."

"The thought crossed my mind, of course, Cinta, but how?" Intrigue had begun to replace all other emotion.

Gennie understood. He was not afraid for his own life. De Xavier loved *Despair* as one might love a child, and his crew, so freshly placing him in command, would judge all future decisions on this most dire. The role of leader was not a lesson she had chance to learn in her journeys.

"I will, if you allow it, return to the archives. There must be something in the papers with the Indian map, perhaps." Gennie shivered, waist deep in the cold water the dim light offering little comfort. She glanced at the carpenters, soaked head to toe, and wondered if they felt the cold at all.

She felt the weight of the captain's coat fall on her shoulders. At her height more than half the garment floated on the surface, the heavy fabric leeching in the water.

"Come on then, before you are blowing your nose in my books." De Xavier put an arm on her and they returned the way they had come. "Back to work men!," the captain barked as he turned away from the carpenters.

Chapter 14

Gennie poured over the volumes collected in the cabin,. sSo many languages, so many sto¬ries, so much information, and misinformation, but nothing in any writing was easily discernable. Gennie had traveled far. By chance, she stumbled upon languages and dialects as diverse as the peoples that derived them. In the company of natives, she could always find at least one with a working knowledge of a language common to both. In a matter of days, she could understand most basic phrases and in some cases speak at a child's level. Written words were easier, as long as the language was Latin based., Eastern symbols eluded her almost entirely. It was not only the languages that confused, however. Sailors were a well- traveled but superstitious lot, so much of what she found was of myth and fear, or rum- induced fantasy.

"The captain wants to know if you've anything yet on the mystery ship." the gunner, Richie, interrupted Gennie's reading.

An energetic and more–than-a-little-psychotic man, with as much love for chains and knives as powder and shot, Richie annoyed more than frightened Gennie, but she was not so foolish to tempt the man's temper.

"I've no interest in what it is, just in how to best send it to the bottom of the sea." Richie rubbed his hands.

Gennie shook her head, "No. I think, if I understand this, sinking her is the last thing we should plan to do."

The statement educed the same response that one might get for taking a toy from a child. "We're not goin' to pay that beast back for the holes it put in us?" Richie pouted.

Gennie smiled and held up the book with the most important and easily translated information. "Tell the captain I need to see him."

Richie did as bid, but momentarily poked his head back in the door, "And you're sure we shouldn't sink it?"

Gennie shook her head again and rolled her eyes at the gunner. The man left the room dejected by the woman's responses.

"Richie tells me you've found something?" De Xavier swept into the room, his demeanor less inflamed than when he visited her last. "Let's have it then."

"Say please?" Gennie teased, but beckoned him over to her side. "Here," she indicated.

The page depicted a drawing similar to the ship *Despair* fast approached. The letters were not a language that either at all understood.

"So you have a drawing, surrounded by other drawings, as far as I can tell. That helps only so far as telling us that the thing does exist, but not much else, and not at all how to overtake it." De Xavier paced.

Gennie opened another book, this one in English. "From the East India Company." She pointed to a symbol at the top corner of the page with the word Junk beside it. With her other hand she put a finger on the previous page, and a matching symbol.

De Xavier looked at the two papers. He pulled the East India Company book from under Gennie's hand.

"I had never heard of such a vessel, and would never have attributed it our opponent if not for that drawing." Gennie crossed her arms. "They are describing the same beast, and now I am certain of something more."

"Certain of?" De Xavier looked up from the book.

"I want her," Gennie stated.

De Xavier lowered the book and stared at the woman. "What?"

Gennie swallowed and again stated, "I want her."

She waited for De Xavier to laugh aloud, tell her no, or simply take the book and walk out. When he did none, she continued, "I want my freedom. I want a crew. I want that ship." Gennie breathed.

At this, De Xavier did smile. "What you ask for is not freedom, only a different cage."

Gennie stared, confused.

"A captain is not the captor, not a good captain at any rate." De Xavier looked Gennie up and down. "Do you think I am free? I am slave to this crew. I am here to protect them, to nourish and clothe them. If the stores are low, it is no one's fault but mine own. If there is unrest, there is unrest because of the captain's laziness or lack-witted motives. I am slave to this ship. I am commanded to have capable crew to man and maintain her. *Despair* and her crew are my possessors, not my possessions," he sighed. "It was what her former captain did not understand, as you witnessed. A crew of slaves will work very hard, for a time."

"I have done as you bid since boarding this ship. Done so, and so much more! I want her." Gennie repeated, undaunted.

"And then they revolt." De Xavier smiled.

"Do not think of this as revolt." Gennie leveled with the man. "There are many unique features this vessel offers. It would compliment your galleon well."

"So, you are telling me that you will act in partnership with Despair?" He seemed uncertain of the truth to the young woman's words.

He also knew that alone, without enough loyal crew, she had little chance of survival. She was a smart woman for all her willfulness, she would not be so foolish as to leave the side of those she trusted, even moderately.

De Xavier nodded, "Then you shall have her, Cinta." Gennie breathed and smiled. "Now tell me the secrets of your soon–to-be prison."

"This reads that the truly large junks were burned by the Chinese government. This one," they had moved to the deck, and Gennie read the description as De Xavier kept watch on the junk's movements, "she is not small either, but I would have liked to see larger."

"She is still quite a catch." De Xavier huffed.

"Oui, mais cette plus la. She is one of the larger sizes listed. Count the masts," Gennie ordered.

"Five," De Xavier replied.

"That makes her over one hundred and sixty-five feet in length." Gennie smiled. "Still, a sea monster. Magnificent."

De Xavier side-glanced from the ship to Gennie. He smiled to see her enthusiasm. "Beautiful."

"The hull is flat. She rides, well, more on the water than in it." Gennie demonstrated with her hand and the book. "But this, the sails, is astounding, and so simple I do not know why all countries have not adopted the style."

"Oh?" De Xavier, proud of his galleon, a ship he worked diligently to obtain because of its greatness.

"Do you see? They are not billowing and full as those of *Despair*." Gennie indicated the sails in turn.

De Xavier had noticed, but thought little of it. A ship could pull her sails tight or let them fill round.

"They are made more like a lady's fan than a western sail, sparred. And they rotate." Gennie paused for the meaning of her words to take effect.

De Xavier lowered his gaze and looked at the page in Gennie's hand. "She can move in any direction, no matter the wind."

"And she is fast." Gennie knew that one would get to him. The galleon was slow and steady, a fast ship could be a threatening enemy or well-suited ally. "But this," Gennie read, "through some science, or magic, of powder and propulsion, the Chinese have engineered a cannon capable of firing just above the surface of the water, able to tear clean, through both sides of a vessel, at the most vulnerable point. The range of the cannon has been tested with complete success at distances as large as four hundred feet." She paused and looked out over the water. "I would say that hit us quite a bit further."

De Xavier grabbed the book from Gennie's hands. "Wonderful!"

"De Xavier, you saw what it did at the distance she did fire. What do you really think a closer range would have done to *Despair*?"

"You are asking us to move against an impossible enemy." De Xavier gauged the woman's emotions.

"Not impossible." Gennie leaned in to read the page again. "Here." She pointed. "It says the cannon takes much effort to load and reload."

"And since the last shot, she has had plenty of time." De Xavier argued.

"Not if she fires again, at a smaller target, and misses," Gennie pressed her plot.

How was it, De Xavier asked of himself, that he had not seen the young woman's skill for other purposes? He knew she was not a navigator, though she had tried on *Lenore* and for the former captain. They too had not seen her for her real asset. He should have guessed from her lineage, but had not considered.

"Why did I not make you First Mate, Cinta?" The captain looked at the small young woman taking in fully for the first time what she could be to him. "Your father would be proud."

The question startled Gennie. "I am sorry?"

"You are not a navigator." De Xavier laughed, "Gods bless it though you try. You have no head for map reading or direction. I worry you will lose yourself on the ship some days." He smiled, genuine understanding coming to him. "You think like a pirate. No," He put a hand on her cheek. Gennie pulled away, though only from instinct. "You are not a First Mate. You think like a captain. Tell me how we are to obtain your prison."

Gennie took a moment to digest the words the man offered to her. She took her eyes away, feeling as though something more might come of this than the acquisition of a ship.

"Because of the design of the junk, even if her water cannons are on her nose, she is still a wider target than the galleon, and she is completely flat decked and low in the water compared to the galleon," Gennie continued. "Chain shots fired will knock the crew covering the decks into havoc. The more crew we knock down the better. It is not the vessel we are out to disperse, but her keepers."

"And if we do gain enough to board her?"

"We will not board like brigands. We will march like soldiers. The decks are flat, like a field. If we drop on her nose, hold formation, we can push the crew into the sea at the opposite end, turning the ship into one giant plank to have them walk.

"It is a bit scary, the way you think, Cinta." De Xavier looked again at the book then handed it to Gennie. "It is your plan and your prize. *Despair* is your weapon. Serve her well."

It took a moment for Gennie to catch the captain's meaning, but no time at all for Talena to understand as she listened in to the exchange.

"You are giving her command?" the first mate glared. "She could ruin us all." De Xavier put a hand on the girl's shoulder.

"You are first mate Talena, as you do for me do for Cinta.

She will serve only as a general of sorts, and only for a short time, that does not make the duties any less." He leaned in to be eye to eye with Talena. "Besides, you will be rid of her if this succeeds."

De Xavier turned away from the women. They two smiled at one another, both awkward at the prospect of the charge they had been given.

"Crew of *Despair*!" De Xavier bellowed over the din of the preparations.

The crew stilled almost instantly and eyes turned to De Xavier, his hands on the rails of the helm brushed the smooth wood.

"I am have reason to believe that our young navigator has a very sound mind for battle." He paused, looked over his shoulder to Gennie, who moved to his side. "Cinta, Blackstrap Gennie, has a plan to capture the junk that dared to fire upon us. Serve her well and we all share in the prize she aims to claim as her own!"

The silence followed long enough to make Gennie uneasy, but De Xavier knew his crew. A resounding 'Aye' boomed from the decks. The war cry was deafening, hands beat cannon barrels, oars and packing wands beat the decks, all manner of whooping arose and certainly carried to unseat the ease the crew of the junk may have felt. Gennie was terrified.

"They believe in you. For now." De Xavier put a hand on Gennie's shoulder. "I expect you to take that piece of junk, and leave my ship in one piece. Understood?"

Gennie nodded looking out onto the crew that awaited her orders.

"Take this boat around." Gennie called out.
"We are going to play a little game of chicken," De Xavier laughed.

"The face of the junk is wide, not like a galleon that has a narrow fore." Gennie laid out the designs and her plans on a table she had requested brought to the helm. "The water level cannons are here and here." She set her index and little finger on either side of the face of the junk. "It takes time to load, light, and fire the device, so if we stay our course the worst we can expect is two shots, one far to the left the other on the right. Our wake should push the things out from the ship, with enough speed."

"And if not," Talena interjected, "what then?"

Gennie leveled with the blonde woman. "It will work, but we will feel a shudder, like before. It will rock the ship. Richie?"

"Aye, aye, mistress," Richie saluted.

"You say that with too much ease, Richie," De Xavier noted.

"Richie, please be certain all of your men know to secure their guns. We do not need chaos on our decks to mirror that which we want to cause on the junk."

"Aye, aye." Richie bowed and swung down from the top rail to the deck below.

"Captain De Xavier, would you man the swivel guns, with the crew not assisting Richie?"

"My pleasure, Cinta. Chain shot?" he offered.

Gennie nodded with a smile. They thought alike. She had been flattered. Now she was honored and amazed. He had faith in her. She swore then that if the day ended as planned she and her ship would repay the kindness eternally.

"There is one flaw in my plan," her brow knit in concentration. "Stopping."

"Excuse me?" Talena looked at her.

"I do not want to destroy either vessel in the end, but if *Despair* is to have enough speed to wake the water cannons askew, the issue will be slowing enough not to bore the junk in two."

Talena sighed, she glared at Gennie a moment before setting aside her anger and concern, "De Xavier trusts you, so I trust you."

Gennie shook her head, "On this point, I do not even trust me."

Talena put a hand on Gennie's shoulder. "Sink my home and I will kill you, but for now I will focus on my part. Explain again this formation."

Eyes wide, Gennie knew the woman was not lying. *Despair* was more than a ship to her. She had been one of De Xavier's first, and as first mate Talena held a love for the ship near equal to that of her captain.

"Right, the phalanx," Gennie explained. "Used most notably among Spartan and Roman armies in the days of the great empires."

"Skip the history lesson."

"Yes," Gennie nodded, "As long as not a single man steps out of line the wall will work. Keep your orders simple directions, switching frontlines out, always pressing forward. We will run them off of their own battleground."

"This is a plan used in land battles though, Gennie," Talena pressed. "How do you suppose it to work at sea?"

"What is a ship, but a floating piece of land, and if these designs are true, the junk is one very large, very flat, piece of floating land."

Talena nodded as she stared at the image on the weathered paper. "Right. Let's do this."

The galleon was slow to speed, but once momentum took effect and the wind filled her sails, faith in the plan increased as well.

"Captain!" the call came down from the crow's nest.

De Xavier did not respond. He looked to Gennie, the same look of pride since the seed of this plan. Beneath the permission to respond something else bubbled, though Gennie did not dare guess what it was. She took her eyes away and to the boy in the crow's nest. "There is, well, it looks like, a fire riding the water's surface," the boy called down.

`"What side?" Gennie called back, then took the spyglass and pressed between the crowd to the bow of the ship.

`"Both, captain, though starboard is closing faster."

`"Aye," Gennie called to the helm. "Ease to port thirty, no, twenty degrees. We do not want to run into the other, only wake the first. Prepare for possible impact!" she bellowed to the crew.

Holding on to all they could, one another included, the crew of *Despair* prepared to be shaken as before. As planned, the first sparkling weapon struck the wake of the galleon and ebbed away for her target. The cylinder hissed out the length of the ship and released an explosion sending a spray into the air around it and a bubble-like wake below. The bubble was what shook *Despair*, rocking her crew on the decks and sending at least one unfortunate soul into the sea.

"Press into the force if you have to. We cannot forget the second." Gennie barely completed her statement when the second cylinder hissed into the wake.

This one, forced even more by the increased wake caused by its brother, flipped into the air several feet above the surface of the water in a vibrant display. It exploded not far enough from the galleon. The sparks flew onto the decks and set more than a few sailors' clothing, hair, or hats on fire.

"Guns!" Gennie bellowed. She was certain they were within range, but De Xavier waited a moment longer, experience giving him more patience.

The chain shot exploded from the pair of small cannons mounted to swiveling posts in the bow. Whipping through the air they made for their target.

"Drag anchor!" Gennie ordered.

They were close enough now to hear the screams and cries

of the junk crew and the horrible splintering of wood and bone. It was the centermost mast that had been struck. Gennie watched with pain in her eyes, the mast, beautiful sails, and masterful engineering, split near its base, topple twisted and roll into the sea, taking with it even more of the devastated junk crew.

"Drag anchor!" Gennie bellowed again.

They were moving too fast, she was sure of it. She wanted to close her eyes. She wanted to block out the impending image of the two beautiful ships tearing one another apart, the bodies of their prospective crew scattering into the sea. She kept her eyes wide, though. A good captain would not look away: she was sure of that, too.

The groan of wood on wood twisted her stomach, but the only cracking was the two foremasts snapping like a knight's lance against one another.

Before the masts fell completely upon the deck of the junk, Gennie gave the order. "Formation! Forward!" She heard her command echoed by Talena and sighed before releasing a wild cry and joining the crew in their spill onto the junk.

It was only after the last of the junk crew fell under bullet or blade or into the sea that Gennie's ears stopped ringing. Her muscles were numb, throbbing with each breath. The stench of death, blood and powder hung over the deck of the junk. Gennie watched as the crew tossed over limp bodies or parts of bodies into the sea. She did not notice De Xavier standing beside her until he spoke and shook her from delusion.

"Her name is *Mei Hei Feng*, Cinta," he sighed. "It is written in scribble and English on her sides. She will need some work before she is seaworthy again. My *Despair* put a few dents in her."

"Her name is *Ecstasy*." Gennie took in the ravaged beauty of her ship in the dying light. "And her captain is Blackstrap."

J. J. M. Czep

Chapter 15

The gangplank bounced lightly beneath the weight of Gennie's more jubilant steps as she made her way to the dock. The air was heavy but served to raise the woman's spirits no less. Mingling scents of sand and salt, fish and damp wood carried on the sea air. Gennie breathed it deeply. Her gaze floated down from the cloudless morning blue to settle on the coastal Topolis. She frowned.

"Not the way you remember it, captain?" Marrick's long face appeared beside Gennie.

"It has seen better days, I suppose." She tipped her hat back a bit to take in the rotting docks and slanting buildings.

Marrick cleared his throat. Gennie turned with her hands on her hips. "The wench auctions are this way, ma'am." He jabbed a finger down a narrow street. "Shall we see if the inhabitants are any better?"

Gennie dropped one arm but offered the other.

"The day is young. The sun is smiling. I think it a fair day for a bit of wenching. Do you disagree, captain?" Marrick cracked a wicked grin, a glint in his eyes.

"Not at all, mate." Gennie jacked a thumb to the empty sky. "Though, I must say I do have a preference for wenches dressed in spring colors on a rainy day all the more."

Marrick shook an accusing finger at the woman, "Some days, I'm not sure who's more the cad," but he took her arm as offered.

The pair made way to the center of the tumbledown settlement. It was not in the least as Gennie recalled the port town. She was grateful in some respect. To return was not her way. Differences made it seem a bit less like going back. She watched the people as they watched her. They knew pirates, knew trouble when it walked. Ten years ago, this wanderer turned pirate captain would take offense to the look in the eyes that followed her through the streets. Maybe the part of her that was Solange was still not flattered, but Blackstrap most certainly was. Arm in arm with the grinning Marrick, who most certainly was proud of the infamy, she could not help but allow a smile to continue to grace her features.

"You!" Gennie halted at the accusing tone projecting from the stout bearded man before her.

Marrick, always at ready for an order of aggression, released the sword from his back. The bearded man stalked up, nose-to-nose, almost level height with Gennie and stopped. Gennie's eyes narrowed grew wide a moment after and a cunning smile of recognition decorated her features.

"It has been a long time, sir. Please, refresh my memory of how we are acquainted." Gennie put an arm on the man's shoulder only to have it slapped aside.

The man removed the shabby tricorn leather hat that held flat his matted mane of brownish hair. "Slasher, do you yet not recall?"

Gennie nodded, "Of course." She opened her arms. "Travis. How could I forget the son of the fine Tavern owner who fed and kept me so well on my last visit to your fine town."

"Aye, and recall you have dues unpaid to me." Travis rested a hand on his sword. "You are here to pay up, right?"

Gennie laughed, "There is some mistake in the books, mon frère. I paid your father in full before I left."

"It is not the debt to my father I speak of, woman!" Travis reddened.

"Oh," Gennie's smile broadened.

"I refer to the gambling debt and stolen wenches, Mad Blade!" The youth fingered his sword.

"Mad Blade?" She put a finger to her chin in thought. "No. No, that is not a name I go by. Is it possible you have found the wrong person?"

She moved to step around the short, round man. Spry for his girth, Travis blocked the path once more, hand full on the grip of his blade now.

"Attendez, I am sure there is some misunderstanding here." Gennie, not fazed by this change in course, glanced at Marrick. "You are much mistaken as to who I am, so I am sure I am just as mistaken as to who I thought you to be." She sidestepped again. "We will be on our way."

"Oh no." Travis pulled the blade free from its sheath. "There is no mistake. A dozen years ago it may have been, but I am not one to forget a face, or a debt."

Gennie held her hand that told Marrick hold his position.

"There is no doubt, you are Mad Blade. There is no doubt you owe me a fight, or a wench and a pretty fair share of booty."

Marrick raised a brow at the proclamation and lowered his guard a breath. "Now, I too am sure there's a mistake."

Gennie tilted her head at her crewman, the smile waning. She rolled her eyes.

"Then allow me to retell the ordeal to clarify." Travis held his ground.

The trio drew a crowd, but in a town seeded with sin and destitution, a pair of blades clashing in the street was barely enough to make a scene.

"As I said, it was about a dozen years ago," Travis began. "A young whelp of a thing is laughing it up in my tavern, dallying with my maids and drinking his fill. All just fine by me, if any coin had been seen," Travis smirked. "Well, I hear this young fool going on, on how he is smooth with a blade. That he can best the best this town can offer. A real mouth runner, like we all once were."

*　　*　　*

"Aye, ladies, as I was saying," the youth in a worn fisherman's hat and coat continued, "I will not hear of it. If any in this town have been cruel to such lovelies I will run him through." He shook a bottle in his right hand, parried with table knife in his left. "I have not gotten this far in my travels without knowing a thing or two."

The proprietor, a younger, though no more clean-groomed man, reached over the braggart's shoulder and pulled the bottle from his hand.

"Aye and I suppose you will do this after you have drunk all of the liquor in my house!"

"Master," the youth rose from his bench, and leaned an unsteady hand on the table for support. "Forgive me, but yes. Before, after, and during if I must. I will take any man."

He offered a hand to Travis, "You may call me the Mad Blade of the Isles!"

"Is that so?" Travis set the bottle to the side and pulled from his belt a dirk.

"Aye, master, and when I best you, I will free your maids here and have the best room, food, and drink in the house!" Mad Blade pulled his French-made main gauche.

The pair circled between the tables. The other patrons cleared out, but only to have a better view. Travis moved with more speed than expected from a man of his size and caught Mad Blade's coat sleeve. Mad Blade took the opportunity, ducking under Travis's arm and, in a move that would pass better on a ballroom floor than a barroom fight, stepped behind his opponent, spun, and moved behind to attack.

Travis quickly grabbed for Mad Blade as the boy slipped beneath his outstretched arm and caught his hat, the audience saw the tumble of brown hair and pretty female face revealed, at the removal of the worn cloth hat.

Mad Blade dove for the nearest table as Travis turned to follow through on his attack. Met with a bottle to the face and a wickedly grinning young woman, Travis reeled from impact and collapsed to the floorboards.

Mad Blade stood over her fallen opponent, "I said nothing about how good I was with a bottle as well, master. For that I do apologize, but still I win, yes? No?"

Travis's eyes rolled as he focused on the shape above him. Regaining some of his wits, he kicked the woman in the stomach, the grin dispelling from her face. "You are a cheat and a wench!"

*   *   *

"Other than that last bit, friend, that is not how I recall the exchange," Gennie said.

"I don't remember that frog tongue you spewed," Travis crossed his arms.

Marrick looked on as the strange pair moved out of the street to lean, or in Gennie's case perch, on a porch rail. He attempted to discern if this Slash was friend or foe.

"And what of the redheaded wench you were all on about, the real reason for the start of the matter?" Gennie tipped her head.

"She was full of herself! She led me on. I let her know my feelings on her behavior," Travis glared.

"More it was that you were hoping to have what was far outside of your reach and, as I recall, it was you who called me the Mad Blade, not I who introduced as such." Gennie leaned forward on her perch, hands clasping the rail.

"You were drunk!" Travis spat. "You were so far into my rum stock you were speaking French and relying on my tables to hold you up!"

Marrick stepped into the conversation. "So did she best you or not, mate?"

"I remember how it was." The tavern owner, Slash's father, stepped onto the porch and into the conversation.

"You were foolish children, both but aye, this one Travis calls Mad Blade, she did win, albeit not as a traditional fighter might've."

Chapter 16

Familiar with sailors long enough to know rum and developed a taste for it, but not near long enough to hold even the meager rations and having grown up on aged grapes, did not make one ready for the ocean's drink of choice, no matter how much one may have imbibed.

Gennie, going by whatever name each crew she chose to sail with chose to call her, still playing off as a young boy, enjoyed the company of tavern ladies. She had an easy way with people, not like the innkeeper's son, Travis, who was typically watching back alley plays, consuming the dregs of what the players considered food for their audience. The night of the squabble, Travis had on his arm a slinky, redheaded lass, taller than he was by half a head and far more than he could handle, though the boy failed to think so.

It did not take long for the wench, drawn by Gennie's easy manner, to join with the rest of the girls in hearing the sailor's adventure. She knew, like a good few of the girls, that Gennie was a woman through the disguise. Half their attention was to keep safe one of their own, though no doubt more than one unwitting young wench will still tell the tale of the sweet young sailor boy that stole her heart that night.

Travis returned from the back room with one fine bottle in the tavern to find his woman, at least in his mind, stolen away by this transient. Travis stalked up to the gathering. Gennie was going on about a past clash of steel. Though most of the telling was in

French, the girls were entertained nonetheless.

Travis put a hand on Gennie's shoulder and an arm around the redhead as he pushed between the pair. Conversation and giggles dispersed, but the smile remained on Gennie's face and was all that could be seen beneath the floppy hat that was a size too large for her head.

"I will wipe that grin off of your face sailor and have your hand, too, if you do not stop harassing my girl here." Travis did like to make himself out the noble of any quarrel.

From Gennie, Travis received only tittering retort in French that might have been something about dogs, Travis's appearance, or both.

"I don't speak frog, boy! But I am fluent in steel. How about we step outside?"

The wench spoke up at this point, "Slasher, I really don't need my honor defended, and we didn't mention anything about being your girl. The sailor was just entertaining us. No harm."

Travis grabbed Gennie's collar and hauled her from the bench. The wenches who knew Travis stayed their place, knowing he would not make it far, but the few who knew Gennie for what she was, at this point a very drunken young woman, followed, including the red head.

"Travis, you best know what you're doin' before you go off on a sailor. Could be he is a pirate!" the redhead called. "Could be he's a better sword than you."

Travis, with little intention of listening at this point, continued to drag the tittering doll, Gennie, into the street.

"On your feet, nave." Travis watched the drunken fool teeter to full height, all of barely five feet. "Draw your blade! If you're sober enough to entertain ladies, you are well enough to play against me."

Proving again, his size would not betray his speed, Travis had the space between them closed fast by the time the crowd gathered. Gennie, still barely aware of the situation, turned, bowed, and doffed her floppy hat at the sight of the redheaded wench striding out to meet her. Gennie drew her blade as Travis's came to occupy the space where her neck had been exposed a moment before. Gennie's eyes were wide at the sudden spark of steel at her cheek. Travis's face was about as shocked to see a woman's face looking at him with a cocky, if not somewhat confused, expression.

It was the redheaded wench who turned the quarrel. Sweeping in behind the smaller woman, she snatched the hand that held the blade and with it parried against Travis. Drunken woman in tow, twirling out of harm, the wench cornered him.

Gennie did finish the job. With the wench herding Travis toward the rail, Gennie swiped a bottle from the nearest hand, emptied the contents down her throat, and brought the vessel down on Travis's unsuspecting head.

*   *   *

"Now! That is more as I recall," Gennie laughed at the older man's telling.

"It was only later that my boy here told the story of Captain Mad Blade, the dangerous, cunning swordsman that stole his wench and pouch of gold. Gold he actually spent on poor plays and poorer food earlier in the night," Travis's father laughed.

Marrick was rolling in laughter at Slasher. "What of the wench that did best the lad?"

"Aye," Gennie smiled, "it would be fine to know what became of her. She had skill unmatched, at least that day, with a blade, and I would be curious to know what other skills she might possess.”

“She’s not really a sword fighter. It was luck. She is just a performer for one of the companies,” Travis growled.

“Her skills with a sword are no act. Classically trained, I am sure of it,” the man’s father gestured to an alleyway. “Shows each evening, there.”

Gennie looked to Marrick. “Shall we take in a show then?”

Marrick nodded and put out an arm to accept the captain’s.

“Hold on! We are not through,” Slasher called out.

His father’s hand connected with Slasher’s skull. “And what will you do? Have yourself beaten again? Be grateful that tall one laughed at your attempts rather than having your head off.”

Marrick laughed again as Gennie pulled him along.

“I like him,” Gennie smiled as they entered the alley.

“Who? Slasher?” Marrick glanced down, confused.

“Aye, him too, but I meant his father. That is one cunning old pirate to have lived this long.”

“And how do you know he is a pirate?” Marrick questioned.

“Woman’s intuition,” she replied and let the silence fall between them.

Marrick rolled his eyes but did not question further.

“This wench,” Marrick asked after a moment, “why look for her?”

Gennie just sighed, “She saved my life. She is good with a sword. She is, as I am remembering, very attractive. Do you need more reasons in answer to a stupid question?”

Marrick shook his head, “Captain knows best.”

The meager stage leaned at the far end of the alleyway in an alcove created by surrounding buildings. The dark velvet curtain draped over the warped crossbeams lunched on by rats and moths.

“How dare you insult me?”

"It is you who have insulted me, sir!"

"En guard!"

Marrick crossed his arms to watch the players rehearse the scene. He enjoyed a good farce now and again. Were he not so accustom to life at sea, Marrick entertained that an actor's life would be enjoyable. He was adept at memorization and thought himself quite funny in games of wit and jest.

Gennie watched for other reasons. Actors were notoriously underpaid, transient, romantic about the sea, and often more skilled than most would allow. The wench was no different.

Her long lean body moved with fluid thrusts, twin blades a part of her person. Gennie observed in silence, inspired by the woman's beauty and skill.

"She's got nice tits," Marrick noted.

Gennie shrugged, "That is true. See there, you did need one more reason."

Marrick smiled as he pushed away from the wall to follow his captain. Gennie applauded as she approached the stage.

"Very impressive work. I hope to stay in town long enough to see the full show."

The redhead turned an inquisitive expression on the intrusive woman. Gennie tipped her hat low and smiled up at the woman a wide foolish grin that most would have been ashamed of in sobriety. Shame was not one of the captain's strong suits. There was ploy to this grin. It proved effective.

The redhead's expression turned to that of recognition, and she dropped from the stage, lithe as a feline.

"Oh well, forgiveness. Oh captain, my captain." She swayed toward Gennie, no question at her movement's motive.

"Aye, and there is the truth of it now." Gennie took her hat from her head and bowed. As she rose, she caught the tall wench's hand in hers and brought it to her lips. "Now it is no lie that I have a vessel that is all my own, and crew and booty to share with my pride."

"Is that so?" the wench gazed down at Gennie. "That would be something I would love to see."

"And so you shall!" Gennie offered her arm.

Marrick grinned as the women approached. Gennie could see the thought behind his eyes but could not make it out in detail.

"Mr. Marrick, is there something you would like to say to my lady and I?"

Marrick bit his lip to stifle the bubbling laughter. He shook his head.

"Marrick, I will have your tongue if you do not start wagging it," Gennie scowled playfully.

"Aye. Aye, captain. What would a cad like me do without a tongue? I will say," Marrick paused, "it's only that I've rarely seen a pirate so small with a wench so tall."

Gennie glowered, "Are jabs at my height all you ever fire?"

The wench, sensing the trouble only in jest between mates, smiled to join the fun. "Mr. Marrick was it? I assure you there is nothing at all wrong about my captain's height. You see," the wench placed Gennie's hat upon her head, "she is perfectly the right height."

Unwarned, Gennie found her face near smothered by the voluminous bosoms of the taller woman. She had no need to bend or stand on toe for the wench to position Gennie in such a manner. When Gennie came up for air, she smiled up at Marrick.

"Aye, Mr. Marrick. I will hear no more nonsense about my height." Gennie shook off impending arousal and hoped she would be right about the wench.

She linked arms with the redhead again, and they continued

their walk to the docks.

"So, my dear, what do your friends call you?" Gennie inquired as they walked.

"You may call me Redd, with two Ds, of course," the wench smiled.

"Beautiful and funny," Gennie laughed. "I like you. I also owe you."

"I mean no offense, captain, but it was not for your sake alone that I came to your aide and bested that fool who calls himself Slasher," Redd smiled. "He has a way with women that I am sure he tells most is quite the opposite of the truth."

Marrick laughed at the statement and tossed a glance over his shoulder at the women. "That is an understatement by my guess."

"It was a pleasure to finally have cause to make his real face known. I owe you, captain, as do all the ladies of that tavern."

Gennie was a bit shocked, flattered, and she absolutely let it go to her head. "It is too bad that I owe you nothing. I have so much to offer."

The trio stopped at the slip that hosted the single-masted fishing junk she and Marrick had used to come to shore. Gennie gestured for Marrick to climb aboard. Marrick offered a hand out to the wench.

She cautiously accepted. "This, captain is your vessel you spoke of?"

"Nonsense!" Gennie blustered. "Marrick," she dropped onto the tiny vessel.

She assisted the wench aboard and settled in for the ride, "raise the sail, and put out the oars if you must."

Marrick shook his head, but did as bidden. The wench sat in silence with legs and arms crossed and a haughty look upon her long pretty face. Gennie stood, one hand on the mast ,trying not to make eye contact and remain as regal in stance as possible. Mature composure was lost as the dinghy rounded from the port cove and *Ecstasy* rose into view.

Gennie bent and wrenched the wench from her seat. "If I can see it, I know you can clearly."

Redd looked out over the water and she did see.

"That," Gennie stood on toes to whisper, "is *Ecstasy*."

"I am sure she is, my captain, I am sure she is," Redd sighed.

Marrick brought the tiny ship around to her much larger counterpart.

"Mr. Marrick," Gennie called below her on the ladder, "when we get aboard you have the deck. I will be in my cabin." Gennie looked above her to watch the swaying skirts of the wench just as she disappeared over the rail.

"Aye, captain," Marrick called up and watched Gennie disappear as well. He did not expect the scene on deck as he pulled aboard.

The uniforms were not familiar to his eyes or expected so far north to those, like Gennie, who did recognize. The crew of *Ecstasy* was nowhere to be seen, save for the captain, at gunpoint a dozen times over, and the newly recruited wench kneeling but in the same position.

"AdeebA Korsana, we are under orders to commandeer your vessel, *Ecstasy*, formerly *Mei Hei Feng*, and all goods aboard and escort you and your crew, alive, to the steps of the sultana M'nef Sheilk's palace."

Gennie looked back at Marrick, then at the wench, and raised her hands above her head. "Not much choice, now, is there?"

Gennie watched the sails rise and fill, which was usually a sight that brought awe to her eyes no matter how often seen. She

122

looked to see Redd's expression and to smile at the woman. Gennie pointed at the bright green silken display above and nodded. The wench's brows knitted in confusion. She would understand soon. There were few events that served to phase Blackstrap's mood.

"So, what have you done with the remainder of my crew, hazarapatish?" Gennie looked up at the stone face of the sultana's general. "I would hope you did not toss them into the sea. I just recently pulled some of them out."

After a long pause, Gennie staring up at him with a look equally cool, "Your crew will be sold as slaves to the many nobles who visit the sultana."

They were alive. That was enough to put Gennie's mind at ease. When she had not seen any but the soldiers, dread and loss at the death of her friends had been hard to cover. Five years of collecting and searching for the lot to at last find the final piece of her plot and lose them all would not be counted as fair by any reckoning.

The hazarapatish stared at Gennie. "You are much smaller than my men expected by how your story travels."

Gennie raised a brow. "Was that meant to be an answer to my question or just a stab at my stature?"

"I do not suppose you would allow me to see my crew, to prove you are not lying of course. I mean what would be the harm? You have at least half your men with you, do you not?"

The hazarapatish strode in the direction of the steps to the lower deck. He did not beckon Gennie to follow, but she remembered the man's manner and did so.

Gennie smiled, "You know your military skills would be welcome on my ship."

"You do not know what it is to quit, do you, Korsana?" the man laughed.

Gennie remembered how his laugh had surprised her the first time they had met.

"For the time it took you to locate me, it could be said the same of you," Gennie laughed along with the hazarapatish.

"We are not allies, you and I, AdeebA Korsana, but I do have some respect for you, if only for your ability to seduce and fool a woman whose mere presence makes most cower."

Chapter 17

"You there! Thief!"

Gennie knew the title was all hers. She darted into the nearest alley. After the battle with *Despair*, her new ship was in dire need of repairs. The closest port city was a shining labyrinth of golden spires and glasslike-globed buildings. Gennie had never seen anything so foreign, and she needed to explore; as expected, she had gotten horribly lost.

The guard was strict here. She knew better than to steal from a people who took your head for looking at them funny, but food was food and the sweets in this city were decadent.

Gennie managed to lose her pursuers, but in the process lost her way entirely. She was far too inland to smell the docks. She was unaware that she, found by other means, would not escape so readily the thousand of the sultana's elite military.

The palace was the only building that stood out as a landmark in the maze of sandy-hued buildings. Bright alabaster walls shone in the midday sun. Gennie dizzied by staring up at the golden spires and banded tower walls. She turned, startled by the groan of the gold decorated oak and iron gates, to the palace parting open.

Curiosity drew her to take a closer look. She should have run in the other direction, down the open path that led directly to the port.

A hoard of soldiers, at least a hundred, spewed from the expanding space in the wall. They surrounded Gennie before she could think escape.

"Are you boys kidding me?" Gennie held her hands on her hips. "All this fuss over un bon-bon?"

She stood her ground even as the giant soldier in gold-accented armor approached and looked down at her. Times such as this Gennie wished to be at least a few inches taller. The man was a wall. Over six feet tall with a shape like a powder keg and likely a personality to match. Gennie could not help but swallow her fear at the sight of the man's hands. He easily could take her head clean off with a single swat.

"The sultana wishes audience with you," he bellowed.

"C'est vrai. What the sultana wishes, I am most certain she may have." Gennie waved a hand to lead the way.

"Is the full escort necessary?" Gennie took in the tapestry-lined corridor as the troupe of soldiers lead her through to the chambers of the sultana. "There does not appear to be many exits from what I can tell."

The general of the guard said nothing, his gaze steady on the direction the group advanced.

Another set of doors as ornate at those at the entrance of the palace opened and revealed yet another set of similar doors. This went on five more times, to Gennie's count. The final set of doors opened in to view an expansive throne room.

Plush jewel-tone carpeting covered the cool marbled grey mosaic floor. Pillars of incense perfumed the corners of the alabaster room, pale smoke filling the buttressed ceiling. The entirety of the militia filled only a small space in the room. Skylight openings were arranged to light the steep ridge of pillows and layered rugs near the rear center of the room and highlight the women seated there.

"Welcome," a voice echoed off the wide air space of the area.

Gennie kept an eye on the pile of women, searching for the keeper of the voice that had welcomed her. A slender, dark-skinned woman rose from her place at the center of the gathering. Her robes were of a material lightly woven to make the wearer cool and the viewer curious of the integrity of the flowing garment. The hue was opaque enough to hide the body beneath the fabric.

"You are the sultana I am brought to meet?" Gennie bowed.

It was better to play the game and keep one's head a moment longer than not and certainly lose before the game began. The sultana's hair was plaited and beaded. Her skin was smooth and beautiful without the use of makeup, though her eyes lined with the kohl of local style. Gennie took in expressions of the women who remained seated when the sultana rose to her feet.

"Is it not typically the men of your culture who keep so many wives at their side?" Gennie asked the dark-robed, lightly jeweled royal.

"It is typical, that no matter the sex of the sultan or sultana. There will be invitation and mandatory participation of as many lovely women, boys, men, whatever the fancy." She waved a slender hand over the red hair of the woman closest to the throne. Gennie took in the woman's expression. "I prefer to keep the women my late husband kept, as they are trained, and collect many of my own ladies too."

Gennie kept a level stare on the sultana. She had a feeling where this meeting would lead.

"I would like you to keep me company for a time." The sultana stepped into the space in front of Gennie. She took in the scent of ocean, wind and recent battle. "First I would like you to bathe."

Gennie made a face at the insult. She did not think she was that offensive. To pirates, sailors, and fishermen she was not.

The sultana said nothing further. She snapped her fingers,

and two large guards took hold of Gennie's arms.

"Hey, now!" Gennie shook and kicked.

She felt the grip on her increase in force. She could feel the bruises forming. She settled down. A bath never killed anyone, and it would give her time to plan escape back to her fallen ship.

The bathhouse took share of the palace, enough to be a palace on its own. Ivory pillars and marble floors shone and reflected the shimmering of the great pools of pale blue, scented water. An aromatic array of petals floated along the mild current of each bath. Gennie was lead by the red-haired woman she noticed earlier, a narrow-framed blonde, and two much larger wives with pale skin and dark hair braided to their thighs. Gennie was more worried about the dark-haired women than the guards that stood at each entrance they passed backs their to the bathhouse interior.

"You don't think I smell that bad do you, bella?" Gennie leaned to whisper in the ear of the redhead.

The woman just looked at her. "The sultana wishes all her wives to smell like flowers. Each of us different."

"Some garden," Gennie smirked. "And does the sultana pick her flowers often, or does she just like to walk over them?"

Gennie was proud of the expression her inquiry left on the redhead's taken aback face. The blonde ignored her altogether.

"You have lost your freedom, korsana, but you are still not afraid or at a loss for words?"

"Korsana?" Gennie tilted her head to look up at the woman.

"Pirate, in the tongue of the sultana. AdeebA korsana was what she told her guards to fetch when she first saw you in the market two days ago."

"Two days?" Gennie was the one taken aback this time. "She watched me wander lost in search of parts for my ship for two days before deciding to reel me in?"

The harem wife smiled, "No. No, korsana, it took her two

days to find you," The woman laughed. It was a laugh Gennie could get accustomed to. "You were lost?"

Gennie narrowed her gaze, "Aye, mademoiselle, I was lost. This place is a maze."

The woman shook her head, "All this time. The sultana thought you a cunning creature to elude her guard for so long. And you were lost."

"Heh," Gennie found less humor in the situation, but it was still amusing.

"Truly?" the woman asked again as she helped to remove Gennie's belts and boots.

"Truly," Gennie shrugged and pulled her blouse over her head. "I was exploring, though unintentionally." She tossed her trousers on the growing pile of steel, leather, and cloth. "It is sort of a talent I have. So what sort of flower does the sultana take me for, if I may ask?"

"At the moment, dear AdeebA Korsana, you are certainly a Rafflesia, for your rarity and all your time at sea."

Genie could sense the comment was not meant as compliment, though she had no idea what sort of flower could possibly be an insult.

The red-haired woman's smile was infectious. Gennie found herself fast attracted.

"Smells a bit like patchouli and orange blossom." She knelt and leaned over the water. The tips of her hair brushed the surface of the water as she took in the scents floating in the rippling waves.

Gennie shook her hair free from the braid that held the mess of dark-straw waves from her face. She lowered into the water, surprised by the warmth, though she noticed the thin layer of steam that floated over the pool. She would not complain about the treatment thus far.

As a young girl, Gennie always enjoyed a warm bath. As a

pirate, the luxury of any bath was rare. She tried to recall the last time she really enjoyed being clean as she sank and allowed the water to envelope her entirely.

Chapter 18

Solange reveled in the warmth of her bath. She closed her eyes to avoid making contact with the maid hovering beside her. The woman's impatience was typical, but Solange knew this time would be the last she would have to deal with the scowling old woman for some time.

"I will be out when the water cools," Solange put a small towel over her eyes. Ships, Solange knew, did not have the luxury of warm baths. She was set to enjoy this one before her adventure.

The maid laid out dress and stockings meant to wear for the day. Solange dressed as the maid packed, but instead of packing as bid for the short voyage to La Rochelle arranged by her father, she included the items she might need for the possible indefinite extended term at sea on *Lenore*.

"All these years, ma chou-chou, you behave not in the least as a woman, and now, when you are traveling and should behave less frivolously, you decide to pack bags more than even your mother carries?" Solange's father laughed.

The girl smiled. Typically, she would pout, annoyed by her father's teasing, especially his calling her a little cabbage head. She knew, though, that this allowance for travel was a fragile one. Solange wanted to see her father in a good mood for as long as possible. She did love the man, but she was no longer a child. At nearly sixteen, she felt capable of caring for herself. She embraced her father, holding on possibly a moment longer than she would on any other day before calling to the footmen to carry her baggage to

Lenore.

"The captain said he will take good care of you. The voyage will be short, but enough for you to experience what it is to be aboard a ship," her father explained as they made their way to the planks of the ship Solange would call home, at least to La Rochelle.

"I am to stay out of the sailors' way and make no trouble." Solange took in the beauty of the ship. "Is that your wish, papa?"

"It is, but you may pester my old friend and captain of this vessel at least a small amount," her father flashed a mischievous grin.

"And what is this look I see so familiar on my old friend's face." The captain of *Lenore* made his way down the plank to the slip. "It is not a look I recall fondly unless I am included on the reason behind it."

The captain and Solange's father embraced. Solange stood beside with folded hands and eyes on her feet. She could play the picture of noble femininity for a short while longer, though the idea was painful as she stood so close to her escape.

"Captain, I introduce to you my lovely daughter, Solange de LeRenard." Her father put a hand across her shoulders.

Solange inclined her head to the captain, a shy smile gracing her young face. Her father had made certain to have the maid make his daughter up that morning as the picture of French nobility and innocence. He knew better of what lay beneath the sweet look on the pale, subdued, round face that peeked beneath neatly pinned, brown tendrils. She was the picture of innocence in a pale blue dress. De LeRenard's daughter was very much the reason for his premature loss of hair and graying of the remaining.

"It is a pleasure to make your acquaintance, young mademoiselle." The captain took the white lace-gloved hand of the girl in his and kissed the fingertips. "I, and my crew, will be most honored to make your voyage with us, though brief, as comfortable and fondly memorable as possible."

Solange smiled in the direction of the captain, but made certain to keep her eyes low. Both propriety and her giddy thoughts made it impossible to look the captain in the eyes.

"Ahoy!" a shout traveled from the rails of the *Lenore* down to the trio on the wharf.

"Ah, and here indeed is another of my crew that will be certain to make it his soul's purpose to make you happy and comfortable." The captain waved a hand at the ship.

From the planks marched a man of such exceeding height that Solange forgot her training and looked up directly.

"So she is like so many women though you taught her well, my old friend," the captain laughed. "Like any other, your young miss cannot look away from my first mate."

LeRenard kept an eye on the approaching sailor, his certainty about the security of his daughter on this short sail waning slightly.

"He is a bit young to hold such a high office, no, old friend?" LeRenard asked the captain as the first mate closed on the three.

"He is," the captain admitted, "but he came to me well-trained and well-recommended. He is not a scholar, to be sure, but the boy can fight like no one I have seen, and he has a mind for command and strategy." The captain turned from his friend to the young man. "Marrick, may I introduce you to my dear friend and once employer, Monsieur de LeRenard."

Marrick returned a curt bow in greeting and deference of the man.

"And this," the captain again took the hand of Solange.

Solange tried to remain in her façade of the demure debutante, but the game was beginning to wear on her nerves. She wanted not to be shown about like a piece of art. She wanted to be aboard ship and in more comfortable attire, eager as she was to sail as a sailor, not as a noble guest.

"This lovely young flower is his daughter, and our guest aboard *Lenore*, Solange de LeRenard." The captain completed his introduction giving the girl's hand to his first mate to pay respects.

Marrick bowed near in half, more out of need due to severe height difference than respect. "And what a tiny fox this fair one is." The young man kissed the girl's fingertips.

The hold on her hand was a moment too long, and the green eyes that should not have dared to look up in the least at a woman out of his class caught her brown eyes for the same extended moment.

Solange tugged her hand away, though it was unnecessary. Marrick released her just as Solange began to feel uncomfortable. It was a sly smile that met her scowling brow, and a knowing look that said he understood how much trouble little noble girls could be and would not dare to be on any ship he held office on. Solange returned a look that bespoke challenge.

"Solange, please, mind your station," her father scolded into her ear as if he had not seen or heard the behavior of the first mate.

He had not due to his concern about his daughter's often unrepentantly unladylike behavior.

"Marrick, boy, you best not get your head into thoughts that could cause the lot of us trouble with this one," the captain ordered into the ear of his first mate.

Marrick and Solange nodded to their perspective masters, but the rivalry had begun in their minds at the very least.

When Solange's father had not sent word or arrived in La Rochelle, the captain displayed some concern, but travel by land could be unpredictable. He could wait another day or so before he would have to leave port to keep schedule for his other expeditions.

"You have been the bane of my existence since boarding

my ship," Marrick barked at the girl.

"It is not your ship," Solange interrupted the man's rant.

She followed the sailor around his cabin as he prepared to take leave with the others.

"I only ask that you take me along this night," Solange begged. "I have been trapped in this small space as long as any, and I wish to see this city before returning home tout de suite by carriage as soon as my father or his footmen arrive."

"If you think for a moment I am taking your spoiled arse with the men tonight, you, lass, are sadly mistaken." Marrick slammed his hat on his head and threw his coat onto his shoulders.

Solange stomped her foot. Marrick stared down at the tiny annoyance.

"Oh. Aye, that will make a lick of difference in your favor," Marrick laughed.

The man turned away and exited the cabin. Solange made to follow, but in two long strides Marrick cleared the stair to the upper decks and down the plank before Solange could further protest.

She pivoted and returned to the small first mate's cabin. Taking in the array of effects still left in the room, she smiled with wicked genius.

Solange, stealing the belt and sword of the first mate of *Lenore*, pulled her boots on and made for the door. She checked her appearance. *Very much a corsair lady*, she noted.

Solange had not a clue how to use the sword at her side. She only wanted to look frightening as possible to scare away any trouble. Making her way to the tavern the others aboard ship had discussed, though not as openly as she would have liked, the girl made certain to pull close the stolen tricorn black hat and dark coat.

It was not until she reached the corner from which she could see the tavern that second thoughts cross her mind. The place crawled with courtesans of every class, sailors, captains, slumming nobility, fops, pirates, and other manner of men that Solange, young as she was, did not know to exist.

She watched for some time hoping to sight someone she did recognize. It was Marrick who stood out to her great relief. Over six feet in height, the man was locatable in any crowd. Solange could see he was distracted, bottle in one hand and buxom wench in the other, but she made her way into the crowd.

With her eyes only for the first mate, Solange's focus was not on the small group moving in her direction and path. Too late she noticed the leader of this pack and collided with the man's shoulder.

"Pas valeur ta temps, monsieur, excuses moi," Solange mumbled a half-hearted apology as she continued on her mission.

She heard the whisper of steel against leather and turned to meet the attack. Surprised by her own skill, Solange's blade caught the offending as it came toward her head.

"T' ose insulter moi?" the man hissed at the girl.

He was well-dressed. Solange took in that much now that she was looking at the man. His ankle-length black coat swung smoothly as it settled from completion of the turn made. Solange found her eye drawn to the tricolor of feathers in the black cavalier hat perched jauntily on dark hair.

She was caught off guard by the man's question, but she could not back down now, no matter she had never really fought outside of a few fencing classes from a traveling tutor that had stayed in one of her father's estates. She had no idea how she had insulted the man.

"Ah," Solange paused, she was not certain how her words heard and interpreted by the man, but by the look of the situation the offense was serious. "Oui. J'ose!" she spit back at the man.

The weight of the sword and the force the well-dressed man pressed into the locked blades caused Solange's arms to tremor.

"No one insults Sebastian Wild Tiger Alison Sebastian de La Rochelle and lives to tell of the encounter!" Sebastian countered.

Solange glanced away long enough to see others of Sebastian's group encircling her and their ringleader. Between the shoulders of the massing crowd, Solange could no longer locate Marrick or the others from *Lenore*.

"Le soin pour le confirmer avec l'acier?" Sebastian made a show of skill and played with the growing audience.

Solange's blade twisted in her hands as Sebastian circled his sword against hers. Solange scowled. The man was toying with her as demonstration to his prowess for the eyes that watched. She could play too, at least with words.

"Évidemment, mieux que tu." She forced her blade against Sebastian's, circling their blades in the opposite direction.

The tall man cackled at her, but waved his free hand at the crowd. "The small one believes she is better than I."

"Oui je suis!" Solange took advantage of the vanity and distraction of the crowd play and pressed forward.

Her height proved both advantageous and inconvenient in the move. She forced Sebastian to release his force on her blade and managed to slide beneath the overhead attack that caught her blade as she raised it over her head. The effect left her and him opposite their starting positions.

Sebastian worked to hide his shock at the bold and unfamiliar move. This girl was either very well-trained or completely ignorant.

"Pas mal pour une petite fille," he called as the girl spun around.

Solange glared, prepared for another attack, then paused. If Sebastian could play the crowd, so, too, could Solange.

She took her right hand from its grip on the sword and placed it on her hip. "Pas mal pour un vilain monkey," the last word blurted from the girl's lips, a broken syllable and heavily accented curse.

Sebastian's eyes grew wide. Nostrils flared, he cursed back at the girl, "Sont des insultes tout ce que tu as?"

Solange broadened her focus to take in the reactions of the crowd. What she saw gave her much more confidence. She stepped out of reach of Sebastian's blade and circled, forcing the man to do the same.

"T'ne sait pas rien ma force," her eyes glittered.

Sebastian cackled again, striking and causing Solange to be on her guard again barely blocking the attack. The man was very good.

"She thinks she has skill, but strikes with insults and jokes," he laughed.

"Mais non, monsieur. I will win this fight." Solange edged her way out of reach and around the ring of the crowd again.

Sebastian raised his eyebrow at the remark, "Vraiment?"

With renewed anger at the girl, Sebastian attacked with two rapid parries. Solange felt the whistle of air from the attacks but blocked both. It was the third she did not anticipate. Blade knocked aside, she leaned back, bent near horizontal to avoid the tip of the blade that paused, still trembling, at her throat. Sebastian's victory and wicked smile were short lived. The click of flintlock and hiss of more than one blade released from its sheath caused the man to look away from his prey.

His crew still circled, though with blades at each of their necks. He discovered a pistol at the base of his skull. He felt the cold barrel.

"Is that any way to treat a lass, mate?" Marrick leaned in close to whisper in Sebastian's ear.

138

The man swallowed and lowered his blade from Solange. Solange returned to a more flattering pose and gathered her hat, which had fallen from her head. Straightening the tricorn on her head, she approached her attacker.

"Vraiment," she grinned.

She looked at Marrick with pride and thanks. The look she received in return spoke of much discussion when they returned to the ship.

Chapter 19

She roused from relaxation to harsh tugging at her scalp.

"Damn it all!" she cried and spun free from her assailant.

"Watch your tongue young woman." A blonde woman Gennie had not seen before held a brush in one hand and a handful of knotted brown hair in the other. "Don't pirates have combs aboard ship?" The woman's tone was meant to be commanding but the pitch of her voice, so strained, weakened the assault.

Gennie glared and shrugged, "'Is my hair lovely?' is not first on my mind when attacking,"

"Sit," the woman ordered.

Gennie did as bid, a shock to herself as much as any in the bath. The brush-wielding assailant continued her attack as if there had never been pause.

Gennie winced at every stroke, "You are pretty brutal for a delicate harem flower."

"I am not one of the sultana's wives. I am Umm to the kingdom's dancers."

Gennie pulled away to look at the woman, "A dancer?"

The woman turned Gennie's face away to continue brushing her hair. "Yes, a dancer, with too many years to do anything else but continue to dance and train the young ones that come to the sultana."

Gennie would have nodded if her neck were not about to snap from the brutality of the grooming.

"I am to train you," the woman scoffed, "though I think it foolish to do so."

"Hey now," Gennie scowled but dared not turn her head, "what does that mean?"

"You will not be here long enough to be any good," the woman whispered.

Allowed to turn her head at last, Gennie watched the woman. There was cunning behind the old girl's eyes that intrigued.

Chapter 20

"Here you are, captain korsana." The hazarapatish waved a hand for Gennie to pass.

She dropped into the opening to the deck below. Startled by their captain's sudden entrance, the crew of *Ecstasy* was on their feet having sat so long in the dark lower decks of the ship. More than a few eyes were wide to see Gennie alive at all.

"Bon soir, *Ecstase*," Gennie waved. "What is this? We have guests and I find the lot of you sitting about?

"I will give you only a short time, korsana, before my men will think me weak and I will have to have you killed," the general called down.

Gennie gazed through the opening from which she had come at the man staring down at her. She nodded with a smile.

"You are bluffing, mon ami, mais, I will not take long."

Gennie waited until the man disappeared and could hear the footfalls fade completely. The man would do much for her in the absence of his ruler, but Gennie knew the location of his loyalties. She would not be foolish enough to trust him. Discussion between captain and crew was not his privilege. She returned her attention to her crew.

"Well," she rested her palms on her hips, "this is a fine way to welcome my new wench aboard."

She paused to scan the poorly lit room. "You do not make your captain or yourselves look competent in the least, my friends. Who am I to blame for this?"

She took in the faces of her most trusted crew, Maggie, Faye, Haitsu, before her gaze fell on a darkened corner of the room.

"Blaze," she demanded.

The tall assassin appeared from the shadows, arms crossed, head low, though the posture was of calm rather than shame.

"I left my *Ecstasy* in your hands." She looked at the man.

His blue eyes locked onto her. "You did."

"You disappoint me, for the first time," she whispered, "but you will have your chance to redeem yourself." To the crew she said, "As will you all."

They were listening. She could sense worry among some, excitement in others.

"It appears an old friend of mine has come calling for me to visit her." Gennie smiled as she paced. "M'nef Sheilk is reigning sultana of a little known port city by the name of Kjoura."

The wave of voices that followed was as Gennie expected. It was Maggie's that stood out.

"Kjoura?" The woman laughed. "Aye, little known indeed."

Gennie shrugged.

"How is it that sultana of one of the wealthiest and deadliest port cities in the Mediterranean comes to know my well traveled captain?" Maggie continued, asking what so many others only thought.

Gennie could always rely on the navigator to speak her mind, and do so with so much knowledge.

"No worries Maggie. I am certain my fame does not outshine yours. Let there be no jealousy between us." Gennie put a hand on her friend's shoulder. "But if you are annoyed by this, I have a present for you."

Gennie reached a hand to the hem of her skirts, lifted the fabric to her knee and pulled from wrapped around her leg,

Maggie's favored bullwhip. Maggie's broad, devilish smile broke free as the navigator took the whip.

"Have you only a gift for your favorite navigator," the woman inquired rhetorically as she bound her leg in the same fashion.

"Non, of course not, bella." Gennie pulled a pale cylinder from her thigh height boot.

"Oh captain, my captain." The wench sashayed up to Gennie's side. "How ever did you know they stole this from me?"

"A captain makes it a point to know the secrets of all her crew, including the newly added, even if others think her to be only a pretty wench." Gennie tapped the end of the device to her cheek before handing the cylinder to Redd.

Redd leaned from the waist to kiss Gennie. She stepped back, and sensing the others desire to know what the weapon was, she took an end in either hand and pulled. The cylinder split at the center to reveal a pair of short, though ferociously sharp blades.

"Where is my favorite rat?" Gennie called out. "Sanji!"

The boy shoved his way to the fore of the crowd, making a point of nudging the cook a bit harder than necessary and pause to smile up at Maggie.

"You have something for me, Yao nuu?" The boy's eyes glittered.

"Likely not as much as you have for me my sticky fingered rat, and that is Captain Yao Nuu, if Yao Nuu at all." Gennie crossed her arms and stared down at the boy.

The difference in height was rapidly decreasing with each passing year. The day would come where the boy would be taller. Gennie could accept the physical surpass so long as he continued to be the one looking up.

"Aye have plenty though not all that you requested, captain." The boy reached into the pockets of his long vest.

Several small pouches of powder, tied tight with fuses attached bloomed from the boy's hands. Reaching into another pocket, he revealed a fist full of throwing knives rolled in fabric. The boy pulled more pocket-sized weaponry from the array of hidden places in the vest.

There was pride in the captain's eyes. The boy was a natural.

"Here." Sanji held out a fist.

Gennie put her hand under the child's and he opened his hand. Gennie grinned at the slightly melted lump of candy.

"Better than good, mon chou chou." Gennie popped the bon bon in her mouth. "Pass those treasures to our dancing girls. It is fair time their costumes are as full of death as well as dazzling jewels. And for you I have one more thing, but you will have to be the one to fetch it."

Gennie pulled a ring of keys from her bodice. The boy's eyes grew wide. Only on special occasion did Yao Nuu allow him use of his favored weapon.

"Do not forget to bring anything else that might be of use, but the bow is the most important. Wear one of my short coats to conceal the foolish thing." Gennie smiled at the boy she was about to entrust all of their lives to. "Now find the place that made you invisible even to Maggie."

The boy snatched the keys with a short nod and scurried away in to the shadows of the room. Gennie returned to her charge of pulling weaponry from pockets and folds of her attire. She handed off a large meat cleaver bound to the inside front of her bodice and handed it to a giddy Faye. Haitsu came forward to retrieve the other whip Gennie snuck in as a belt. Gennie sent up silent hope that Marrick would acquire at least one sword on his own before turning at last to Blaze.

"As I said," Gennie stood close to the man looking up into the only slightly averted blue eyes, "I am gravely disappointed. I did have much faith in you. Fortunate, I still, and always will."

Gennie reached into the front of her bodice. She waited to be certain the man was watching. From her cleavage, she revealed a small gold-barreled, ivory-handled, pistol. Blaze's eyes lit as he watched the weapon waving before his face.

"And to prove my trust that your pride will induce you to redeem yourself, monsieur, I have something that belongs to you."

Gennie took the assassin's hand in hers and placed the pistol in his palm. She closed the long slender fingers around the gun before taking her hands away. Gennie turned only a quarter from Blaze before she felt a hand on her shoulder.

Blaze took Gennie's left hand in his. The captain felt herself locked, as Solange had once been, by the assassin's stare, unable to move or protest. She felt the band of metal, warmed from her bodice, slide to the base of her ring finger.

Gennie closed her hand, the gold pistol, hanging from the trigger guard wrapped around her finger, fit into her palm.

"It has been yours too long to take it back." The assassin released Gennie from his gaze.

He shrugged and stepped away to reach into his boot. "Besides, I am not entirely useless." He turned the trio of rotating barrels on his most formidable, though least stealthy, weapon along his arm. The Italian-designed tri-shot, a deadly piece of engineering, weighed far more than the tiny close range pistol and could fire in succession or simultaneously from the long barrels.

"You have a way of ruining a moment, monsieur," Gennie sighed.

She slid the pistol from her finger and returned it to her bodice. The crew of *Ecstasy*, following their captain's example, made the gifts invisible beneath clothing before the guard returned to take Gennie to the deck.

"You spent your time wisely, I trust?" the general inquired, assisting Gennie from the hold.

"Of course." She smiled.

The hazarapatish closed and locked the door to Gennie's cabin closing out her grinning face.

Gennie watched the strange glittering city enter into view. *Ecstasy* made fair time, better than the sultana's navy anticipated. It was beautiful. She wished her crew were on deck beside her to see it this way, the only way truly to take it in, as they came into port. She knew that it would not look the same once behind her this time.

Her attention was drawn away, by another sight just beyond the curve of mountainous terrain that created the secretive port of the sultana's empire. Flicking in the wind, a black tongue of a waiting serpent, the first pirate flag her young eyes had seen so many years ago. It had been the inspiration for her jack. She could not see more than the tips of the masts that supported the faded black sails of the Spanish galleon, but it could be no other ship than *Despair*.

Gennie's eyes flicked to the guard that stood in for her shadow for the duration of the voyage. His eyes would not betray a secret he wanted kept even from one he shared secrets. Gennie would wait. She learned patience at sea more than any other skills. Patience and stillness were like the ocean before a rage.

Chapter 21

"I do not want to go back, AdeebA." the youngest of the dancers that chose to follow Gennie so long ago had a stern, but still frightened look in her brown eyes as the crew marched down the plank to the waiting guards.

The girl was not more than twelve, born a dancer, looked and moved like her mother who trained her, and likely would never have had a dream of any other life had Gennie not stolen the lot of them away from the sultana, but with the taste of freedom came a desire for it. Gennie lifted her gaze beyond the girl to find others. She found the women near to the edge of the group. Typically dancing, always playfully witty eyes, dancers, adapted to the pirate lifestyle with more ease than most. The look upon their faces begged to know how the captain planned to get out of this mess a second occasion.

Gennie smiled and nodded at the women, reassurance and a cocky knowing in the look that bespoke of plans in the hatching. They relayed the same look, but the woman glanced at the youngest daughter. Gennie had no children of her womb, but she did feel a mother's troubled thoughts. Her crew were her children, especially the young ones. Gennie was harsh with them at times, but there was more love in her moments of rage than in the sultana's moments of love.

The palace loomed as it had the first time she had seen it. In the stretch of time, little had changed where Gennie had changed much. She would not allow her crew or herself to be held by this selfish, royal.

She could not help but smile and allow her eyes to take in the glowing walls, plush tapestries, and rugs that enveloped her and her crew as they followed through the palace corridors. Taking in the riches that surrounded, there was a small part saddened they would destroy them.

There would be no other way. The sultana was not one to give up easily. Ten years of tracking a ship with more speed and guns than most, through waters that reached as far from her domain as any, was proof enough. Gennie would not have peace until the sultana and her kingdom found burial.

Gennie took stock of those surrounding her. The gunner, his face as calm as Gennie's, would not betray fear lurking beneath the surface. The man would be eager to plot the cleanest way to wipe the palace off the landscape if he did not have one already. The redheaded wench stood beside him. Gennie recognized budding romance between them. She could not be jealous. She could not deny they looked good together.

Marrick's eyes pointed straight ahead. Though in his mind, his hands wield a sword, Gennie knew. He was ready, too ready possibly, but that was what she needed. The assassin claimed the space to her right, his face hidden by the high collar of his coat and fingers twitching to grasp weapons. He asked so often why she trusted his loyalty. In moments such as this, she could not doubt. He would not look at her, but Gennie could sense he would fight Marrick for the head of the first of the sultana's men to lay a hand on his captain or the crew this loner began to consider family.

Gennie felt her eyes well with pride at the sight of the young crew she sometimes doubted, but she would not allow it spill over. The dark-skinned Jamaican mountain girl, a thief when first met, with lips always eager with chatter that made the captain's head ache, Haitsu's head held high, an almost regal air.

There was no look of the young scullery with a wicked aim and romantic thoughts of seafaring behind her eyes as she marched with the others. No doubt, the girl would wrestle any number of guards surrounding her. She was keeping her lips still, but thoughts were running.

Gennie thought of the little cabin boy, whose antics were the only cause for Gennie to rant about the lack of discipline aboard ship. She threatened more often than not to toss the blonde-haired runt overboard, but counted herself grateful at this moment she never had. The little animal would be a man to contend with in only a few short years, and for now, he no doubt sought to hone skills on the men who took his home and family.

The former wives most impressed. Fighting for more than Gennie's freedom, the fire was in their eyes. Demure ladies, taken from the palace so many years ago changed under the sea's tutelage, into hard, skilled, wily pirates. Nothing ladylike slipped through the looks they threw at the guards they once called protectors and captors in the same breath.

"This will be a short visit," Gennie said to no one and all her crew at once.

"You may hope." The head of the guard looked down at Gennie as they waited for the final doors to open.

"AdeebA Korsana," the sultana's voice boomed from the far end of the throne room, just as the first time. The woman, surrounded by wives and pillows, stood, and airy cloth flowed around her.

"You have not changed since last we met." The woman held welcoming hands out to Gennie as she approached.

"And you have aged twenty years in ten, I see." Gennie smiled as she took the woman's hands in hers and held them, not in adoration for an ally long separated but to ensure the sultana could not strike her for her words.

"Your tongue has grown more fierce," The sultana growled. "Do not forget that it is I who holds you and your crew captive, not the other way around."

Gennie released the sultana's hands when the woman tugged at the grasp. They stood for a time saying nothing, only weighing the other. The sultana was first to turn away. She strode back to her place among the pillows, sat, and smoothed the fabric around her.

"Sit." She tapped at the place beside her.

Gennie did as prompted. She made no move to look at any of her crew. She looked at none in the room other than the sultana. Her jaw set, her entire body ready for what might come. The game had begun. Every move would count.

The cushions were as plush as Gennie recalled. The aroma of the garden changed only with the replacement of certain missing flowers. "You must tell me all of your adventures," the sultana coaxed. "I am certain you have seen many things. Have my wives and dancers behaved for you?"

Gennie knew a loaded question when she heard it. "My crew listens well. Of course, I try not to give orders that would be seen as foolhardy."

"Of course. Of course," the sultana smiled.

Gennie spoke again, this time with much less subtlety. "A good leader knows how to please her followers so that they are eager to please her. You will see firsthand, your wives and dancers make commendable pirates."

The sultana darkened. Her teeth bore in a vicious smile, but did not bite. She, too, had changed, more calm than when they last met. Gennie was enjoying this game.

Gennie waved a hand at the woman and sat back to lean on her other arm. "Why send for me, Sheilk?" Gennie asked. She used the informal name of the sultana, knowing it would grate the woman. "Why not have me killed by the soldiers," she emphasized the point with a hand across her own throat, "you sent to drag me back? Take your women back and have the boys here bring my head in a sack. Hells," Gennie jabbed a thumb over her shoulder, incidentally pointing inland, "add the ship to your fleet and my surviving crew to your slaves."

Sheilk allowed Gennie to finish her flourish before placing her hands on the pirate's folded knees and leaning over to come face to face.

"Korsana, you think too little of my ability to rule, to command, to think." Sheilk remained calm though Gennie could tell it was a struggle. "The plans I have for you require your big head to remain on your arrogant shoulders." Her lips were nearer to Gennie's ear than she would have liked even a lover to be without consent.

Gennie twisted her head and glared at the sultana, brown eyes burning into grey. The pirate turned her lips toward the thin lips of the sultana. She put a hand behind the woman's head; guards moved to remove the offense but were halted by a glance from their leader. Gennie grinned at the act of trust and breathed out. "The way I hear it, I think quite correctly about how you think. I know you Sheilk, as you wanted me to know you."

Sheilk struggled away, losing her composure for only a moment, to escape the grip of the korsana.

Gennie laughed as Sheilk pulled away, enjoying the scowl on her narrow pretty face.

The sultana regained her composure and clapped her hands. The dark woman who stood was familiar to Gennie as one she had left behind. Gennie watched the reactions of other wives in the room. Meryem held scrolls in her arms. Meryem bint Tariq, not wife nor dancer, she was adviser to the sultana and wife to the sultan before.

"You do think much like the sultana, korsana, but it is my plans that should interest you now." Meryem handed one of the scrolls to Gennie.

Chapter 22

"How is it that a pirate is able to dance like a Bedouin after so short a time at learning from harem girls?"

Gennie was shocked to hear the woman speak while Sheilk's attention was drawn by girls bringing in large trays of fruit, cheeses, and cooked meats. Most of the dancers had no fear of speaking to Gennie in the days forced to share their quarters. The women, particularly their Umm, Badrea, did not fear Sheilk either. In the harem chamber, the sultana rarely entered. They were free to say what they felt. While they could not escape, some had no desire to leave; they were able to live in their own way.

The wives were very different. Few were ever out of the sultana's sight. They were quiet, most out of survival, but some, like Meryem, were so well-trained to be silent that the idea of speech to any save their sultan was foreign.

"You ask very intelligent questions." Gennie leaned closer to the woman. "You should do so more often."

Meryem bit her lip and leaned away. Gennie grabbed the woman's wrist before she could stand to leave.

"Stay," Gennie pleaded, but followed with jest. "I cannot follow if I wanted." She pulled at the heavy chains that led to the iron brace shackled to her ankle.

The leash was long enough to reach the carpeted dancing area and back to the pillows near the sultana but no further.

Meryem relaxed. "She will see us speaking." The woman nodded in the direction of the sultana.

Gennie gazed over her shoulder, "Aye, I am certain she will notice us, when she is not drooling over the fresh meat that wandered in."

Meryem could not hide her grin at the pun. "You do not care that you are a prisoner? You are either quite foolish or you have a plan to free yourself."

Gennie leaned into the pillows, her hands behind her head. "Neither really. Not yet, but I am working on that last bit."

Meryem shook her head. "You are astounding."

Gennie blinked and shook her head. "I will take that as a compliment though, from the tone, that is not how you intended it."

"She will have you killed before you are out of view of the palace walls," Meryem said.

Gennie sighed, "Well, then, maybe I am growing accustomed to a cage I will never be free of. Is that not what you are doing?"

Meryem looked from Gennie to the back of the sultana's head. "I am waiting," she paused. "I outlived the sultan, I will outlive his head wife, and then I will try to teach the next to behave like a human and less like a vengeful god."

Gennie turned her head to look at the sultana. "Did you try to teach her anything?"

"Yes." The woman looked at Gennie and sighed.

"You didn't do a very good job," Gennie shrugged.

"She takes what she wants. Any woman she finds intriguing she sends her guard to fetch," Meryem explained.

"Aye, that I noticed." Gennie pulled at the chain again. "Please, tell me what she finds so thrilling about me, and I will be sure to strike it from my being."

Meryem shook her head at the small pirate. "For one so slight you speak very plain and think very large."

Gennie leaned forward and onto hands and knees before the woman. "And for one much more beautiful and much larger than I, you behave like a mouse."

Meryem frowned, "I know my station."

"Humph," Gennie sniffed and pushed away from the woman.

"And you will soon know yours," Meryem stated in a tone of knowing. "She will break you."

Gennie crossed her arms and fell into the pillows. "Pas cette âme, belle. I think it is you that will one day soon change."

Chapter 23

"I will admit," Gennie smiled at Meryem, "I am surprised to see you alive."

Meryem said nothing. Her voice, once trained in silence, would not betray her feelings about seeing the pirate caged a second time. Her eyes, though, said much and more. The golden irises cursed Gennie for her capture. *How could you be so foolish,* they screamed. Gennie replied with her eyes in turn. If Meryem taught her anything, it was to say much in silence.

"She is alive because she understood you better than the others." The sultana put a hand out to the woman. "Even though she did aide in your escape, she proved the value of her life with revelation of things you taught her, or so she claims the ideas and information to be yours."

Meryem did make Gennie nervous, that much was true, but only due to what she might have said to the sultana about their conversations.

"You tell many stories, korsana, and speak highly of your crew as well as other captains and their ships." The sultana paced the room. "You are a valued source of information, as long as that information continues to flow from those pretty lips."

Gennie sighed, "And all this time I thought this would be torture."

She watched the woman's face for some sign of

understanding. There was none.

Gennie continued, "As much as I know you love to hear yourself talk, I thought I would be forced to endlessly listen. But, if I am the one talking, then that might not be as bad as I feared."

The sultana's nostrils flared. Gennie flashed a smile. The enraged woman slapped the smirk from her face. Gennie rubbed at the growing redness and shifted her jaw, but the slap had not moved her from her place.

"I could get to like that too, Sheilk," Gennie hissed.

Sheilk's lips were a thin, hard line of frustration at the pirate. It was Meryem who spoke, however.

"Korsana," the woman beckoned Gennie's attention.

Meryem knew Gennie enough to understand that no matter the rank of her offender or if she was outnumbered, it would not keep her from going to blows with the sultana.

"Korsana, please, this could be a most profitable arrangement for all parties involved," Meryem offered.

"Arrete," Gennie held up the hand not massaging her face. "When you say all parties, I have to assume that there are more than just the sultana and myself, non, Meryem? Else you, being a stickler for correctness in all things, would have said both parties involved."

Meryem watched the eyes of the cunning korsana captain. The years had made them both stronger in will as well as body. She was nearer to being the woman's equal in this game, but she could not be so foolish to think herself superior enough to be lazy in her moves.

Meryem looked to the sultana, her orders not clearly written on her features, and Sheilk would not speak through her fury. Meryem would make the decision and accept the consequence.

"You listen well," Meryem inclined her head, "too well at

times. I will be more aware of what I say to you and how I say it."

"You are the same, bint Tariq, and I wager we will equally share the burden of staying on our guard in this exchange." Gennie could not contain her emotion at finally meeting with Meryem on an even field and with Sheilk as witness to the woman's intelligence.

"Agreed," Meryem cleared her throat. "Shall I continue?"

Gennie waved a hand and crossed her arms.

"There is another ship the sultana desires to include in her growing fleet. Loyalty from two captains would be ideal. Though wisdom rests in knowing how pirates behave." Gennie raised an eyebrow and winked as Meryem continued. "*Ecstasy* is only one of the great and much feared monsters on the ocean, dubbed unsinkable, if ever a shot is fired with enough fortune to come within striking range of the vessel. Faster than her counterparts by a far stretch even in winds able to slow other ships down. Cursed, or some say blessed, by demons, able to breathe fire from every side, and in possession of a weapon so fierce it is said even her wicked captain has not fully unleashed its power for the fear of it."

Gennie was grinning uncontrollably, looking from the sultana to the royal adviser. "Oh, no, please, go on," she waved at Meryem.

Sighing, Meryem shook away a grin before continuing. "However, the sultana knows what others in the seas do not."

The sultana interrupted, teeth bared, "*Ecstasy* was not always in the possession of the AdeebA Korsana. So, how is it that such a creature was tamed?"

Meryem waited to be certain her mistress would not say more or strike the pirate a second time. When Sheilk paced away and Meryem was certain Gennie was paying attention to her words again instead of plotting Sheilk's demise, she continued.

"It was with this knowledge the Sultana of Kjoura, M'nef Sheilk, arranged to search the seas for the truth to the legends, the origins if you will, of this mythic captain, crew, and vessel."

"I am certain she was pleased with the origins she discovered," Gennie eyed Meryem.

"Very pleased," Meryem nodded. "The ship that made its mark upon the hull of *Ecstasy* has a name to reflect her adversary and short time sibling, *Despair*."

Though she knew in her heart that it had been De Xavier's galleon stationed at the entry to the port, to hear the name made assumption into fact.

"*Despair*'s legend is near as impressive, if not more so, for the mysteries still unanswered." Meryem looked through the papers in her hand.

"S'il te plait," Gennie rolled her eyes. "Do not say such things so loud with the man so near. His ego inflates so easily."

Meryem bit her lip. She had met the man, Captain De Xavier of *Despair*, and she had heard of his proud nature, well warranted though it was, but stories did no justice to just how extraordinary the meeting had been.

Chapter 24

"Blackstrap Gennie?" There was a tone of insult, though he worked to feign ignorance to the name. "I do not know of whom you speak."

"Is it possible you might know her by a different name?" Meryem could not look the man in the eyes and remain focused on her questioning.

Years of being under the heavy hand of the sultana weakened her resolve. Meeting the korsana had brought much of it back, but this man, this pirate, took it all away again with a look.

De Xavier laughed and sighed. This questioning had gone on too long for his tastes.

"You do know of her then, sir." Meryem drew the pirate's attention back to her.

"Aye." His deep eyes locked with Meryem again making the woman feel a chill to her bones not felt since the sultan was alive.

"Solange de LeRenard was a good name, Gennie suits her not at all to my ears, Mad Blade, I did hear her called on one occasion. Blackstrap is as vulgar as she hopes it to sound and again not suitable. And, what was it that your queen named her?" The man searched for the answer in the arches of the large room. "AdeebA Korsana."

"AdeebA Korsana is less a name than it is a title, sir," Meryem corrected, though a part of her felt wrong to do so. "It means the noble pirate woman."

"It has been some time has it not, Cinta." De Xavier crossed his arms and whispered into the rafters of the room.

Meryem fought the urge to ask questions that were not on her list but to her were much more interesting.

This was a man of power with an empire not yet fully in his command, and Meryem could sense the decisions of her mistress. Sultana M'nef Sheilk would lay out for him the path to that control. Meryem wanted to leave the room, to leave the city, after only meeting the man for moments. She was becoming more certain with every word of their conversation that it was not M'nef Sheilk in control of this man's destiny as the sultana so arrogantly believed. To the contrary, this Captain De Xavier seemed to pull the strings of his own destiny with more skill than the fates.

"It is the desire of the sultana to locate this woman pirate." Meryem could feel herself fighting not to behave childishly fearful of this man.

"And what is the desire of your sultana if she does locate Cinta?" De Xavier continued to stare through the woman sent to create an alliance with him on behalf of her mistress.

He was fast growing bored with the situation, though he felt this would be more to his profit than the selfish wench with a title and palace that had not yet introduced herself.

"The korsana owes M'nef Sheilk her life as well as the return of stolen property," Meryem said as bid, though she could sense the pirate did not believe her words.

"Your sultana misunderstands the term pirate if she believes she will retrieve any of her property, no matter what it might have been. And she wildly misunderstands the nature of the prey she hunts if she believes my Cinta will give up her life without taking more than a few along as her entourage to hell."

De Xavier laughed. Had it not been in her offense Meryem felt she would have liked the sound that filled even the large room they sat in the center of. She could not hide the shudder elicited by the man's ominous words and the amused tone by which he delivered them.

"But," De Xavier continued, "there are reasons why I was chosen for this hunt and I would like to know what those reasons might be. What laudable skills does the sultana believe me to possess that she would find so useful in this game?"

Meryem licked her lips and flipped through the book in her hands. "Your ship, a very large galleon of Spanish origins, heavily gunned and impressively manned with some rather notable names in piracy, yours being most notable, of course, captain, was responsible for the capture of *Mei Hei Feng*, the original name of *Ecstasy*."

De Xavier closed his eyes. He nodded, "Yes. It was *Despair* that was able to win that battle."

"The sultana believes that *Despair* is the only ship and you De Xavier, the only captain capable of capturing and taming *Ecstasy* and with that bringing to her the korsana Blackstrap Gennie."

The pirate laughed again when Meryem finished.

"Your sultana needs to understand the facts of that exchange." De Xavier stood and crossed his hands behind his back. "*Mei Hei Feng* was hung up on a reef, her speed so legendary of no consequence, with a half-starved crew set on survival or mutiny. Hungry, too, with their usual lust for blood. She was limited on ammunition and foolishly wasting what little she did have on passing ships that might get close enough to ignore her." De Xavier sighed and shook his head. He smiled at Meryem. "*Mei Hei Feng* was a sitting duck waiting to be plucked and boiled, if not by *Despair* then by another. *Ecstasy*, she is none of those things."

Meryem listened and noted all that the captain said before asking, "This may be true, but it was *Despair* that did it, no other, and *Despair* did not sink the offending vessel or make off with her cargo. Instead you took *Mei Hei Feng*."

"No, my lady, Cinta took *Mei Hei Feng*." De Xavier shook his head to think of it. "She was the captain that day. She made all decisions. I was proud, do not think I was not, to see my incompetent navigator take over as strategist."

"I am sorry?" Meryem was confused.

"Blackstrap," De Xavier translated the name. "She wanted the ship, and I allowed the girl to take command and capture her prize using my *Despair*. Therefore, while I approve of, and am in complete agreement with, the rumors your sultana has heard pertaining to me, my ship, and my crew, you have heard facts and understand that there is, in reality, nothing *Despair* can do for you. The exchange was fate, and thinking on the part of a member of my crew that no longer sails with *Despair*."

Meryem was running short of things to say to persuade the man. She would resort to the standby when dealing with his sort.

"There is a payment in it for you." Meryem pulled a loose paper from the pages of the book.

She handed the leaf to De Xavier. His interest in this venture piqued once again, De Xavier took the paper and read. After a long moment Meryem cleared her throat. De Xavier did not look up from the paper.

"You can read, sir, correct?" Meryem inquired. She knew that some sailors were illiterate.

The question drew the man's eyes from the page in a cold stare.

"My apologies," Meryem bowed.

"I am not like most pirates, my dear." De Xavier rolled the paper and, opening his long grey coat, slid the scroll into an inner pocket. "Your sultana's terms interest me. The prospect of pursuing, for profit, what I have been does appeal."

Meryem stared at the man. "You would have done this for

nothing." She queried.

"No," he shook his head, blinked contentedly and smiled, "not for your sultana, not for nothing."

"But you just," Meryem protested.

"What I said was that it will be good to continue what I have been, quietly pursuing, going my own course, only now, with more money to be made, and more access granted me and *Despair*." De Xavier's pride was evident. "*Ecstasy* is still my prey, only now I may allow the sultana a time with her."

"That is well enough, I suppose." Meryem was sliding into her shy silent self.

"Have the supplies granted taken to *Despair* immediately, half of the gold promised as well. I will allow the sultana to keep some of her offering until she has *Ecstasy* in her hand. The letter of marque, I will have before we sail."

Meryem caught herself mid bow and stood erect before she embarrassed herself any further. She left De Xavier to consider the terms he had just agreed to.

J. J. M. Czep

Chapter 25

Gennie grinned, "Oui. I am in agreement with you, old friend, but it was amusing the look on her face, no?"

The general shook his head and continued the remainder of the walk in silence.

The pair tossed Gennie into a cell at the far end of a hallway and clanged the cell door behind her. "I will see you soon, hazar'," Gennie called from the floor of the dimly lit cell.

The man did not turn around, but Gennie noted the curt wave of his hand. She still had allies, though the numbers dwindled as they were locked away or swapped sides.

Gennie made her way to the small lumpy cot against the wall of the cell. She hopped onto the edge and flopped across the mattress before immediately taking to the floor again.

"Have you missed me, poppet?" Marrick laughed from his place on the cot.

"No more than I am a poppet," Gennie hissed. "How is it you are in here with me?"

Marrick stretched into a sitting position on the cot and swung his long legs to the floor. Where Gennie's feet had dangled off the edge of the bed, Marrick's knees bent up uncomfortably.

"This reminds me rather of how we met again, aye poppet?" Even in the poor light Gennie could tell the man was smiling at her with that wicked, charming grin.

"That doesn't work on me, if it ever did, Marrick." Gennie paced the walls of the room taking in the surroundings. "Why put me with you?"

"I suppose our dear friend and guard of the sultana did not wish for you to get lonely or die of boredom before his lady called for you again," Marrick grinned.

"Lovely." She rolled her eyes, but the jest was at least in some ways close to the truth.

Gennie looked through the bars to send a silent thank you to the general. The man was a fair liar, but his loyalties were true, and they were with her.

Gennie pulled the few papers she kept from the sultana and Meryem from her blouse.

"Have you a light in here at all, mate?" she asked.

Chapter 26

"You're as cold as I remember, dear Solange." The former first mate of *Lenore* held out the large and nearly empty bottle of rum.

Gennie knew from the moment the possibility of having her own ship presented itself that she needed to locate Marrick and have him as her first mate. She did not expect to find the man a drunken waste of his former self.

"You will call me Blackstrap." She snatched the bottle from his hand.

Rumor of *Lenore* traveled to Gennie as *Ecstasy* sailed nearer French ports. The trail came to rest with a story of how the first mate, a man once thought destined to carry on with the crew of *Lenore* became a drunken sot.

"The name doesn't suit you," Marrick belched.

Gennie shook her head at her old friend, one she once looked up to. "You have not seen me drink."

She pulled the man from the bench, not an easy task with the height difference. To see the man standing she realized just how much she had forgotten his height.

"LeRenard, that suits well, my fox." Marrick teetered as he leaned down to Gennie's level.

From the corner of her eye, Gennie caught a gaggle of scowling wenches. The group watched Gennie from the moment she entered the pub.

"And you, sir, are a hound as I recall." She put hands on either side of the man's face.

"Of course. You wouldn't have me any other way," Marrick blathered and rested his free hand on the woman's shoulder.

Gennie sighed as she slid alongside Marrick to heave him off the floor again. "LeRenard is my family name. It should still suit me, but it is not safe to use."

Marrick set the bottle to his lips again and poured the last of the liquid into his mouth. He slammed the empty on to the table and waved to the innkeeper as Gennie lead the man out the door.

"You are cunning, quick, and quite a hard catch, LeRenard," Marrick laughed as he allowed Gennie to lead him down the street.

Gennie sighed and shifted her weight to keep Marrick on his feet. "I am no catch at all for most."

"Aye." Marrick was on his knees in front of her before Gennie had chance to react. "I'll 'ave you, poppet."

"You are drunk, monsieur." Gennie put her hands on her hips and glared at the man.

Kneeling as he was, Marrick was eye to eye with his fuming new captain.

"Aye, it is." He grabbed her hands in his, surprisingly quick for one so drunk. "How lovely our children would be."

Gennie pulled one of her hands free to slap sense back into the man, but held back. The line was actually a fair lead to what she had come to discuss with him.

"My crew are my children." Gennie put the hand meant to assault the man instead on his shoulder.

"I recall a saying much akin to that." Marrick thought back to the captain of *Lenore* who lost his life protecting his crew during the attack from *Despair*. "And this crew of yours, it's a small brood yet?"

172

Gennie was not certain Marrick's level of sobriety allowed understanding of her statement, but she continued. "I am rebuilding. We hire hands when we have need, but my trustees are few. The assassin, he is a dangerous one when roused,"

"Assassin!" Marrick's senses snapped a bit into place with mention of the Italian he made Solange swear never to speak of after the once meeting.

"Oui." Gennie moved past the topic, "a good navigator of course,"

"Of course." This changed Marrick's mood some. "You should've a navigator before all other crew with your sense of direction."

Gennie laughed at the insult. At least she had the man's interest. "A cook, too," Gennie continued. "She came with the ship."

Marrick was laughing again. "Aye. That is another position best to fill early on. Is she beautiful and talented in the kitchens?"

As they spoke, Gennie felt something quieting in the little town. The hour was late, this was true, but not so much to have the street rolled up.

"Marrick?" Gennie whispered to the former first mate as she put him back on his feet to continue their walk back to the dock where Maggie waited in a small boat to return to *Ecstasy*. "How long have you been in this town?"

"Aye, lass, long enough to make name for myself, but not long enough to make much money," Marrick laughed again.

Gennie heard the locking of triggers and drawing of swords before surrounding them.

"Un nom," she nodded.

The local guard encircled.

Gennie, chained to Marrick, looked over her shoulder

toward the dock in the opposite direction.

"You had best be worth the trouble you are about to cause me, Marrick," she hissed at the man.

"Lass, this happens to me all the time." Marrick looked straight on. "Never lasts long. I'll get us out."

The guard shoved the pair into the small subterranean cell at the end of a row of buildings.

"Mr. Marrick, I am thinking you will hang for this list," the guard sniffed and turned away.

"Never lasts long?" Gennie raised an eyebrow at Marrick. "What has become of you?" She held up a hand. "No. No. This will end well for me with my crew waiting for my return, but if you want to leave along with us you will have to make a promise to me."

Marrick had sobered enough to see masterful cunning behind the eyes of the once young girl he barely recognized now.

"Aye, did you say Blackstrap was your new name?" Marrick sighed.

With a blade, he could always best the girl, but not when it came to a good bargain or an unfair wager. She would always win, and this time she had the hand of the law to assist her, at least for the moment.

"I need a first mate I can count on." Gennie put a hand out to the man who once trusted her and, with a bit of time, felt could trust again.

Marrick took the offered hand. "Well, lass, that's a better offer than expected, though not the sort I ever thought to agree with you."

Chapter 27

"So, now. How are we getting free of this cage?" Marrick circled the room. "No bars to bend and plenty more guards."

Gennie watched the man. He had a plan, she knew; he always had a plan. Even the one time she saved him, it likely was not necessary, though it was nice to have at least that one time.

Bow across his narrow back, arrows gripped in his teeth, and a coil of rope wrapped the length of his torso, the boy, Sanji, scurried to each of the small square openings checkering the roof of the block building. Looking into each hole, he stopped above the scene searched for and laid the arrows beside the opening. In silence, he removed the bow from his back and uncoiled the rope from his body.

Gennie, standing at the center of the cell and watching Marrick make a show of tapping on walls and peering under the pair of cots, felt something above her head. She looked up through the opening above in time for several feet of rope to fall square on her face.

A gathering of young girls, former dancers, some worth a fortune in the coins they wore, marched up to the only entrance in or out of the block building.

"Through the front door ladies?" one of the guards mocked. "You were planning to take the korsana right out the front door?"

"How did you escape your chains?" the other guard observed leveling a pike at the group.

The first guard did the same in effort not to appear

delinquent in thought. The girls tittered and giggled at the young guards.

The gunner waited eagerly in his assigned location for signal from Sanji. His explosive mind burned to light the fuse and witness the outcome of Marrick's plot.

"We are going to pay a visit to a certain pirate captain if my figuring is accurate." Marrick tied the rope around his waist and tugged.

Gennie ran into the man's arms when beckoned. "You keep your arms around me tight, mate, and your hands from wandering," she commanded when Marrick pulled her close and wrapped the rope around her as well.

"This could only work por vous." Gennie squeezed her eyes shut.

"Aye, poppet, but I only do it to impress the ladies." Marrick mussed the woman's hair.

The cabin boy's eyes focused on his first target as he drew back the bowstring. The first arrow sailed over the roofs of a row of closely packed buildings taking with it the end of the rope.

The gunner listened to the whistling snap of rope as the arrow struck the wall inches from his shoulder. He stepped away and eyed the scrawled stick figure image of a man juggling three cannon balls.

"The kid is pretty good." He breathed a sigh of awe and whistled.

He walked the match over his fingers, struck, and put the flame to the fuse of the small langshe.

Sanji's second and third arrows left the bow in unison.

The girls remained at pike point, though the soldiers commanded they enter the building. The sound, like the crack and squish of an opening coconut, drew their attention from weapon point to the pair of soldiers, each now with a rainbow-feathered arrow sticking out from the top of his head. The soldiers stood for a moment more, one opening his mouth as if to speak before crumpling to the ground.

Marrick gripped Gennie tighter to him as his feet left the ground. The pair sailed through the sky from the propulsion of the fire-spitting missile, through the small opening. Sanji hopped clear of the wildly waving rope tail.

Their path took them over rows of small houses with little enough power to the missile to carry them into the air above the garden pool of a mansion in the shadow of the palace.

Redd watched the langshe as it spit and sizzled directly at her. She set her feet wide on the narrow rail of the high wall allowing the missile to sail between her knees, pulling her double blades and sweeping them together, as if scissors, to sever rope from missile.

Marrick and Gennie, bereft of their ride, fell to splash into a lagoon-like pool at the center of the garden.

The gunner's ears perked at the sound beyond the wall. "Guess my aim is not too shabby either." He sauntered out of the alleyway to meet with the others.

Gennie sputtered as she fought her way to the edge of the pool. Marrick was waiting, his long legs able to reach bottom sooner than the captain's.

"Why here?" Gennie coughed the words out as she shook off the water.

"You'll see." Marrick tipped his head in the direction of a door to the main part of the building. "We'll be surrounding. I've to let the others know we made it."

Marrick stepped over a cluster of short palms.

Gennie looked at her reflection in the pool.

"Not exactly your best look." She turned from her sopping image to the door indicated, shrugged, and entered the archway.

Gennie took in the surroundings as she made her way down the hallways of the magnificently decorated building, passing several empty rooms. She looked into each room briefly as she passed.

"Must be guest accommodations," she whispered to herself.

It did not take long to discover what Marrick had brought her here to find. He had his back to the door, but Gennie recognized the dark hair and sweeping black, sleeveless coat.

"De Xavier." It was a question as much as a statement.

The man spun. His hand on his sword, he faced Gennie. He would have had the blade drawn too, had he not recognized her.

"Cinta?" De Xavier opened his arms.

The captain approached to embrace the soaked and disheveled woman in the entryway. Gennie put up a hand to halt the man.

"I was building a magnificent crew to be in awe of before the sultana made her call," Gennie stated. "Nearly completed a five year process."

De Xavier's face was a muddle of emotions: pride, sadness, joy, amusement. Gennie's was less muddled; anger and frustration commanded her features.

"I am here on business De Xavier, as you were," she scowled at the man.

"Say that yet again, my dear, but in place of business let us put pleasure." De Xavier blinked slowly at her. "And what makes you think I was here on any particular venture, Cinta?"

"I remind you, De Xavier, from here on you will refer to me as Captain, or Blackstrap." Gennie crossed her arms.

"Aye, Captain," his tone teasing, but he was listening.

"And, I know the sultana called you here, with less force than persuasion, because you have knowledge of how to overtake my *Ecstasy*," Gennie pressed the man for more information.

"You know too well how I work, Blackstrap," De Xavier sighed. "It's true. My hold is heavy with offerings from this sultana. I told you long ago, it would give me pleasure to see you in shackles made to fit your wrists exclusively."

"And, as I recall, I swore such a thing would not happen, though I would enjoy similar pleasure to see the same for you," Gennie shot back.

Their battles had always been thus, more words than blows, always a hint of something more to the stinging verbal fire. The flash in their eyes, was not one of animosity. Kinder words, left unspoken between arguments, were vocalized through body language.

"The sultana wants more than your ship. She desires you, Cinta." De Xavier's eyes softened only for a moment.

"I know this," Gennie shuddered. "I know she wants to cage me like the rest of her pets, but I am not so easy to tame."

"I know it." His look said more.

Gennie ignored the man's tone. "She is trapped, as much as you once told me any leader is, by her position and her power. Her frustration comes that her cage does not float."

"She is bored, this is true," De Xavier laughed.

The man was closing the space between them. This time with more subtlety.

"Cinta," the name was all but a curse this time as it sprang from his lips. He caught her arm. "No games, I have missed you." She shook free as she met the cool gaze. "Do not be a thorn in my side."

"S'il tu plait, Commodore," eyes flashed but lashes fluttered, "let me be a blade instead." She whipped her skirt around to reveal a garter glittering with a small steel blade. "And that is not the only one. My blades, my guns, my crew, my *Ecstasy*, yours to command.”

Her words made his eyes glitter in frustration. “A mad blade or a fox, noble pirate or a black strap, you have gathered more than a few names, making you very difficult to track.”

He hissed the words out, “Wait… commodore? Such flattery.”

“Ah,” she clapped her hands together and pulled them to her chest, “so he does listen.”

“Why?” His expression, still cautious, softened some. “Why join the sultan’s fleet?”

“Why ever not? My titles are lost. I am no longer a lady. I am getting too old, and too good, to remain a sailor hopping ship to ship. I am the pirate, The Captain Blackstrap Gennie.” She lowered her skirts and raised a hand out to the man. “You are not my enemy.” She touched his hand with gentle fingers. “Give me a new title, and maybe you can make a countess of me, just a little bit, once again, a countess of the seas, along with your title as king to the sultana.”

The request confused him. She continued, seeing the loss, “You need a fleet for your part in this plan, do you not? My ship and crew are at your call.”

“Cinta, I would not ask you. Even with the sultana’s money, my intent was not to have you kept for very long, just enough to make my duty seem completed and yes, to watch you suffer a bit for your arrogance, but nothing more.”

She put a finger to his lips. “Hush. That is why I offered.” She waved her hand. “Besides this folly, no more than any other risk my crew has wagered, you have not been near me for a few years, De Xavier. I have seen and done much more than the whelp you gathered in your nets. And this particular venture does hold a special thrill for me.”

She wandered about the room taking in the treasures that surrounded them.

"Cinta," the name was less an offending curse this time, "I do need you."

She turned to find his expression sobering. "Then you shall have my allegiance." She strode to him and put out her hand once again, this time as an offering.

"I would wish that I had more than that. I wished so since the day you stepped upon the decks of *Despair*." He kissed her fingertips instead of shaking on the deal offered.

"For that, Commodore, you will have to continue to wish, and request, because I will never offer. You know better than that."

He shook his head and released her hand with a smile. He did know better.

Chapter 28

"What are the sultana's plans?" Gennie moved past De Xavier and into the cabin. She stared down at the maps and papers spread across the broad oak desk she remembered so well. "How many ships has she?"

She looked up to catch the disapproving gaze. "How many ships have you, commodore?"

De Xavier smiled. For all his games, this woman knew him well. She knew how to get under his skin or into his heart and when to do either or nothing at all.

"Gods bless it, how you vex me." He strode to the table.

"Here." Gennie took the tied stack of papers offered. The commodore continued, "Letters of marque, from different kingdoms, ships offered by each, and notes for use in trade with any port from here to the end of the known world."

"Well, they did think of everything didn't they?" Gennie grinned, unfastening the ribbon.

"Cinta," De Xavier put a hand on hers, "do you remember our first meeting?"

Gennie looked into the man's brown eyes, eyes with a depth about them much the same as her own, "Aye, of course I do. Likely not well, but that is not for lack of the importance. I have met many in my years at sea and there is a story tied to each." She smiled at the thought of all of them. "Yours, though, yours is scarred deep in my memory."

"About that," the man cleared his throat. "I never asked for you to stay after finding your *Ecstasy*, for all I did for you then, and all you did for me, I counted us even in the eyes of the gods. It was not because I did not want your ship alongside mine."

"That is why I offer it to you now," Gennie smiled. She had gone over this meeting in her head, but in person, things were not always as imagined.

"Because, I never ask for anything, I demand it. Why can I not do that of you?" He stared at the woman but answered his own question. "I gave reason for you to want to go your own way. Now, though, I am glad to be a part of something worth much more." De Xavier took his hand from Gennie's and put it to her cheek. "Cinta, no Solange De LeRenard, I thank you for not making me ask, especially a young girl."

"The girl is gone." Gennie leaned away from De Xavier's hand. "And this woman, was well taught to make demands."

"I am learning this," De Xavier looked away. He gestured for Gennie to return to the papers.

"But if she were not, she would gladly accept a sincere request, and grant anything as she has already offered, to an old sea devil." Gennie breathed so as not to release the dam of emotions she was working to maintain. "This pirate, though, Captain Blackstrap Gennie, she will tell you there is never anything to forgive or forget and that allegiance offered comes with the price of equality. The sea is a harsh world, and the lessons taught are harsher still. They serve to hone the blade, temper the steel, strengthen the prow and make the pirate worthy to serve in a fleet as masterful as this one shall be." Gennie turned De Xavier's face to hers. She saw something that looked to be some mild emotion, but said nothing. "This woman thanks you."

"You were always right," De Xavier sighed to return his composure.

Chapter 29

The captain tipped his hat back on his brow to lean closer to the bars of the brig. In the darkness, his aging eyes could scarce make out the huddled shape of the captive.

"We will see what we will have of you in the morning," he growled. "For now, let us see how you fare sleep with the rest of the bilge rats."

He paid no mind to the small stone that struck between his shoulder blades as he turned to ascend to the deck. Like any other rat stowed aboard his ship, a bit of spunk meant for a hard worker and trusted crewmember in the end.

"Did you get a word out of the whelp, sir?" the officer inquired as he passed the wheel to the captain.

"Nay." The captain checked their course. "Like as any other, only sticks and stones for being offered this chance."

"Shall I?"

"Bring the little beast some jerky and a spot of rum and water," the captain offered before the officer had finished his inquiry. "None of the good stuff though, mind."

The man nodded and made for the stores.

The captive continued half-heartedly to hurl a few more handfuls of what she hoped were stones at the captain's back when he turned away. She hoped her sex not discovered. Bad enough to be among completely un-trustable men of few morals, being found a woman aboard such a superstitious lot that privateers were, she would be in for worse treatment than had thus far been served. Solange wondered what had become of *Lenore*.

She instinctively wrapped the tattered scrap of blanket tighter around her body at the sound of approaching footfalls.

"Good evening, rat." The face of the officer appeared at the bars, a bowl and flask in one hardened hand. "Captain says to fatten you up before we have you for breakfast."

Solange lunged at the offering only to have it snatched away teasingly.

"Wretched whoreson," she hissed.

"Even a dog knows better than to snap at his master." The man made the offering again.

Solange took the flask first, and politely. Drink was more value than food. That much she learned quickly. She drank greedily of the sour liquid and thought about the number of ships brought down prior to *Lenore* by this singular galleon.

"I did not cut that to be had without food. Eat before you are worth even less than you are now come sun rise."

"Who are you to tell me how much I am capable of drinking?" Solange howled at the man. "You know nothing of me. I have drunk rum of a higher quality than this swamp water, and cut not at all."

She took the bowl of jerky, which might as well as have been leather.

"He intends to have me work, c'est vrai? As a navigator I suppose?" she dared to ask.

"If you can work, for all your slightness. Navigator might be the only decent position for the likes of you," the officer smirked. "You are a runt, now, aren't you?"

"My slight body can out work your swaggering arse on a keg of grog or nothing at all," she spat at the man.

"At least you talk bigger than most on this ship." At that,

the officer left the way he had come. Solange took another long draught off the flask before capping it and tore into another strip of jerky. Sleep came quickly despite the accommodations, though she could not be certain if it was due to the rum or fatigue of the day.

"You're soft. I wonder if they had you work at all on that fat merchant tub," the captain turned the captive's chin roughly in his large hands, "but you are trainable."

The captain had woken his newly taken captive and would be crewmate at a later hour than most of his crew. He hoped to find Solange cowering after a night of unrest, but instead had to kick the creature out of a sound and peaceful sleep.

"I will go far easier on you, if you promise a fair ransom as the son of some wealthy, land baron, you so nimble jumped a ship to be free of," the captain joked.

The captain received a stone-faced stare for the query. Solange knew it might be a way off the pirate vessel if she did admit her origins, but it was not worth the risk. Where would she go?

"Very well then." He yanked Solange up by one spindly arm with a hand that easily encircled the limb. "To work," he paused, "unless you would rather I see you off my ship now, the offer to join Davey Jones's crew in place of *Despair*'s still stands."

Solange had a look near fright for the first time since walking aboard the privateer's galleon. She shook her head feverishly.

The captain nodded and continued to drag the girl to the deck. He dropped Solange at the feet of the man who offered the rum last night.

"I leave this one to you, De Xavier," the old captain laughed. "You were so eager to whip this one, whip him into shape as a formidable sailor."

De Xavier scowled at the annoyance, but nodded acceptance of the task. "Very good, captain."

"If you are mine to train, then you will be mine to command as long as you are on this galleon." De Xavier dragged Solange down the stairs to a cabin filled with books and charts. "You want to be a navigator. Get to it. But first you will have to organize the mess left by the last one."

Solange stared at the disarray of papers and books and scraps of maps. It was a challenge, true, but it was better than being on deck hauling line. De Xavier shut the cabin door and locked it from the outside.

"You will thank me for this later, girl," De Xavier called through the keyhole.

Solange shook the doorknob. He knew, she thought. Her mind raced as did her heart. How had he known that she was she when the captain had not? How many of the others knew, and why had De Xavier kept it from the captain?

Solange bumped her forehead against the door and rested there a moment. She backed away at the sound of gunfire and screams.

"Are we raiding another ship?" She ran to the window.

She could not see another ship. She had not heard the cannon fire shots to signal they were in pursuit. Solange pressed her face against the glass and worked to look up the side of the ship to the decks above. Her angle offered nothing until a man, his body limp and bloody, tumbled over the rail and slid down the glass in front of Solange's eyes leaving a smear of blood down the window.

Solange jumped away. She looked at the door. Deciding the lock was suddenly not nearly enough to keep her safe, she snatched the heavy oak chair and dragged it in front of the door.

It was over in less time than the terror made it feel like, Solange knew. She waited for a time following the silence. When no one came for her, or her head, boredom took the place of fear.

Solange rolled up her sleeves, tossed her hat into the chair at the door and began the toil of organizing the room. with hesitance at first, she took care with one or two maps or books, then more. She nearly completed the task when the sound of a key scraping in the lock drew her attention and set her back on her guard.

The door banged against the back of the chair. Another bang had the chair on its side and skidding across the room.

"So much por le barricade." Solange dove under the large oak desk, taking with her a small gold blade.

"I left you in here for your safety." It was the voice of De Xavier, but Solange did not move from her place. "It would make little sense to kill you after that, don't you think?"

Solange said nothing but knew there were few places to hide. The sound of De Xavier's boots were easy to follow as he crossed the room directly toward her.

"Humph." Solange listened. "You did a fair job cleaning my chaos. I am impressed." De Xavier looked around the room. "And you did this with the noise of killing directly above and all around you."

Solange had not thought about the sounds since beginning her task.

"You are tougher than I thought. You have me hoping you are not worth a ransom." De Xavier stood beside the desk.

Solange saw the rum bottle lower into view, though she continued to grip the small knife, ready for whatever trick the man might pull. She read the label, her name, Blackstrap, was on it. This meant her other articles had been rummaged through, unless *Despair* had a stock of the Jamaican rum as well. Solange doubted so.

She reached out and took the bottle. Then De Xavier's hand came into view, offering to help her to her feet.

"I did not know if you had skill to fight," De Xavier smiled, "but I see you at least know which end of a blade to hold."

"Do you think it is time we were properly introduced?" he asked.

Solange looked at the bottle in her hand. "Blackstrap, like the rum."

The man laughed, "Well, at least your name is on all the bottles." He held his hand in greeting. "Maxmillion Adolf De Xavier, Captain of *Despair*."

Solange looked the man up and down. "Mutiny?"

He nodded.

Solange uncorked the bottle with her teeth. She spat the cork into the corner and took a long swig. De Xavier watched the small woman drink. After a moment, Solange wiped her face, and thinking about the situation, offered the bottle to the new captain.

De Xavier accepted the bottle and raised it to the woman before drinking.

"You are sweeter when you are drunk, Cinta."

"Et vous etes somewhat charming. What does this mean?" Solange asked, taking the bottle back and another swig from the private stock of dark rum.

De Xavier snatched the bottle from her, "That is mine now you know. What does what mean?"

"Why did you betray him?" Gennie held out a hand for the bottle. "The name, Cinta, what does that mean?"

De Xavier took another deep drink, swallowed, and sighed before handing it over. "You are too young to understand. Maybe you never will have to. I hope at least on my ship, you never will. And the name, it means strap, or ribbon."

"I am with you, captain, and the old captain, he meant nothing to me. But the truth, was he as vile as your actions allude?" Gennie tipped the end of the bottle up. "There was no sign of villainy to my eyes. He was a hard man, but not unkind to his crew, for a pirate. He was not the one who wanted to beat me."

De Xavier snatched the bottle away. "Not hard enough. He was a danger to the assets of this venture." He drank.

Gennie could see the sorrow though the new captain would not show it outright. De Xavier enjoyed his service alongside the former captain.

"Pirates do not have the luxury of old age, Cinta." He drank again. "Enough. I want to know about you. I kept your secret from the crew, from the captain. I want to know where you really hail from. I want to know if I should send you back there or keep you on with the others."

"It is good to hear there are other women aboard." Gennie stole the bottle. "There is nothing for me to go back to, but I am from France, as you guessed by my accent. My father was a merchant, quite wealthy."

"A French merchant's daughter, is what you really are?" De Xavier could not hold back the laughter. "Accompanying your father on his outings to the docks, fascinated with the smell of sea air and stories about treasures filed down the gang planks from far, exotic lands, tales of pirates and kraken, filling your foolish head."

"What of it?" Blackstrap pulled the bottle from De Xavier's reach and took a second swallow. "Father always offered some small trinket to console my curiosity, but it only served to feed desires. Solange de LeRenard, though I have collected many names. Madblade is one."

"Madblade? So I have heard of you," De Xavier laughed as he made the connection to a story an islander had retold. "Where did such an elegant creature get such a name?"

Blackstrap laughed at the sarcasm meant as flattery. She followed it with more.

"My enemies know me by my sharp steel, wit, and nails." Blackstrap poured more rum down her throat.

"For a lady with French heritage, the pseudonym is clearly not." De Xavier was enjoying this game.

"I am no longer French so it matters not at all." Gennie swirled the remaining liquid in the bottle, her mind sobering.

"Oh?" De Xavier was not certain what had caused it, but the mood had shifted.

Chapter 30

Wholly unaware to the reality of ship life, Solange had spent several days staring at the sea, not in joy, but in anguish, sacrificing most every vile thing dried and boiled fed to her. Her stomach adjusted after making the first port after La Rochelle. It was at this port she learned that going home would not be an option and getting used to the pain of seasickness would be the least of her pains to accept.

During the month, the inquisition reached her home. Her family, her home, all was lost, burnt, and stricken from record; the same fate had fallen on all Calvinists. She drowned her sorrow in rum, the favored drink of those at sea, and the sights at each port, thankful that the captain of *Lenore* did not dispense of her in some slave auction or brothel.

Chapter 31

"We were quite well-off," Gennie explained.

"And then?" De Xavier felt the girl's story might be similar to his own, but he said nothing of his past.

"The Church burned everything." Solange looked into De Xavier's eyes. She could see a similar pain, but she knew he would not let on, not this time.

"Your family?" De Xavier hated himself for asking even as the words crossed his lips.

Solange's eyes welled, though she fought.

Chapter 32

"I was right only as often as you. Of course, I am now. Shall we skip to the planning?" Gennie smiled, "We have much to do, and I am not certain how secure my crew have made this humble station.

"A woman your age should be thinking of family, not plotting." De Xavier posed the same question long ago.

"There is nothing for me to go back to, commodore, stop trying to tempt me into the safety of a past that does not exist and a future I have no desire to attain. Since my first day on *Lenore*. My family is my crew. My home is my *Ecstasy*. The only god I have ever trusted, the sea, she is honest about her fickle nature."

De Xavier gave the woman a gentle smile. "Fine."

Gennie felt the smile return to her the same feelings she once had for the man who had given her more than a ship. A fair chance ten years ago meant so much.

"So what is the future today, captain?" The commodore crossed his arms.

Gennie smiled the crooked smile, warning that only trouble could come next from her lips.

"What say you to forgoing the addition of such a dismally arrayed kingdom to the list in your hand?"

"I am listening, Cinta. I always am."

Leaving Blaze and a handful of others behind, the crew of *Ecstasy* moved in the dark streets of the sultana's city to aid in Gennie and De Xavier's journey to the docks away from the luxury of the mansion given to De Xavier by M'nef Sheilk.

The pair ordered nothing left behind small enough to carry. When De Xavier turned a final glance over the barren rooms, there was a sort of pleasure glinting in his eyes. For too many years, he had viewed the solid immobile structure as freedom from the risk of the sea. The truth was clear.

Taking all charts, books, and plans was Gennie's quirk, no different from any other dealings. Her arms overflowed with the final books. She looked with wild eyes at De Xavier.

"What treasures you have been holding from me, commodore!" She allowed the man to take some of the load from her.

De Xavier took everything of value by monetary standards, but he smiled at the woman knowing that she shared his need for knowledge. "I beg your forgiveness, captain."

"Your crew is as fine as you say in terms of theft," De Xavier marked as they made back to the ships. "Silent, efficient, strong, very well-trained, but this reminds me, this assassin." De Xavier asked as Gennie helped him to lower the small boat into the water.

"What of him?" Gennie eased her end of the ropes hand over hand watching the shrinking deck rail and the closing waves alternately.

"He is so cold to you, all business. Is the man made of ice? To be surrounded by death so often, it must make him uncomfortable to be around, and yet you spoke of him more fondly than the others." There may have been jealousy in the man's voice, but Gennie did not take it to heart.

"He is surprisingly lively when aroused, I assure," she joked.

"I will ignore that. I suppose he is protective as well?" Gennie, confused by the man's tone, kept her hand steady on the rope.

Gennie let her end of the boat drop gently into the water. She gauged the look in De Xavier's dark eyes. "You hardly need worry. He does only what is told. And yes, De Xavier, I will even order him to silence you if need be."

The pirate nodded. "Good," was all he said.

"They will not disappoint you, De Xavier," Gennie assured the man.

She was not facing *Ecstasy* as the oars dipped into the waves and pushed the smaller boat between the two ships. She watched *Despair* as she spoke. For the second time she was leaving the galleon she called home for a short time. It felt like her first safe haven in the entire world. Even *Lenore* did not tug at her heart like *Despair*. She hoped this would not be the last time she walked the smooth decks. Gennie cursed herself for not taking in more of the sounds, smells, and sights of the galleon. It could all be over after this venture.

"You do not sound as convinced as you are trying to make me." De Xavier caught Gennie's eye. "Do you not have faith in your own crew, captain?"

He was baiting her, as he always did. "More faith than I ever had in yours, captain."

"Commodore," he corrected.

Gennie rolled her eyes and shrugged. "Of course."

The commodore's laugh echoed off the walls of the cove.

Gennie called up to the decks as the tiny boat bumped against the side of *Ecstasy*. She stood on the rocking bench to reach the ladder tossed down. Gennie did not have to look behind her to know that De Xavier was grinning and considering a comment about her height. Ten years, and that, too, had not changed.

Gennie was not shocked to see much of her crew gathered on the main deck to see her return. She looked across to the eyes of her closest, Blaze, Marrick, Sanji, Haitsu, Maggie, Faye, Redd, beyond them a score of others who gave so much to join a ship and captain drawn to trouble. They awaited orders even as they sized up the man adjusting his hat and coat behind her. They were ready. De Xavier may have questioned Gennie's faith in her crew, but there was not a doubt in her mind: her crew was ready for whatever the sultana fired upon them.

"*Ecstasy!*"

De Xavier looked at Gennie from dusting the wrinkles from his sleeve.

"We have seen many strange things in the ocean. We have sailed further than any, of that I am certain. The homelands of this crew stretch to every corner of every sea. We speak as many languages as might exist in the world, for all I can be sure. Our skills are as varied as they are great, and my faith in you is as solid as your faith in me has become. You know me by names that in some cases even I do not know the full meaning. Nevertheless, we have come to speak one language, the only one pirates need know: treasure and freedom. Our adventures will be greater after today. Moreover, our reach will be further still. Today, we join *Despair*." She waved a hand at De Xavier. "We join the fleet of Commodore De Xavier. Today we take the Kingdom of M'nef Sheilk as our home port, and we will not stop there." Gennie marched along the line of crew. "Load the guns, ready the dragons, raise the sails, and let fly the Absinthian Skullerfly!"

She completed her circuit face to face with De Xavier. "You best return to your ship, unless you are going to allow your first mate to give the orders to your crew. I will have one of my men return with you."

De Xavier did not move. "I failed to realize until this point," he beamed. "I had not heard you give orders to a crew since obtaining this boat."

"Junk, commodore," Gennie corrected.

"Aye. You have improved." He turned to leave.

The compliment was small, a breath of appreciation. She dared not grin too broadly.

"Commodore," she had to know. "Before you are off, before the sea separates us, before we throw ourselves into this battle, that, aye, there is possibility, though small, we may not see another day," Gennie held her breath a moment before asking. "I never once lost hope that you and I would be allies stronger than any. We are siblings, you and I, though not by birth. You said that once, and I believe it. I believe we will one day bring down heaven and hell if need be, or just for the amusement of the battle."

The commodore nodded before turning away and making for his *Despair*. He always left her, even in her highest moments, with the feeling that she spoke more than she should. Gennie did not care this time. She said her peace and it was true. If she should die this day she would die with nothing kept from the man who taught her what a captain should be.

Gennie turned attention to her crew, busy at tasks she had not yet ordered but knew needed to be done. Gennie stood a moment with her hands on hips.

"Cela va être beaucoup d'amusement." Her heart raced at the coming battle. Her many names and each part of her person waited.

Solange wanted to run to the foremost rails of the ship and watch, on toes, the fire and splash, hear the explosions, and dance with glee with each victory, and to cringe for every poor shot or enemy's hit.

Gennie composed, though not by much. Her mind eagerly developed new strategy to adapt to each failure, no matter how rapid, with more enthusiasm than skill, but the spark was still there.

AdeebA Korsana felt the vengeance about to reap, all the while her thoughts dipped in and out of concern for the appearance of herself and her ship. A pirate's and a woman's most powerful weapons were her ability to look the part and reputation to make others think twice before encounter.

Captain Blackstrap stood her ground a moment more, surveying her floating kingdom, once and possibly always, her cage. This is no different from any other attack on any other port city, she thought. Nevertheless, she knew, as she looked over the rails of *Ecstasy* to the raised flag of *Despair*, this battle would be very different. Turning to the towers and walls of the sprawling kingdom, this was not just any city.

As one, girl, woman, and captain, Gennie strode to the fore of *Ecstasy*. Her hands on the smooth wood of the rails, she waited for her first to join her.

"Captain," the man asked, "You sure this'll be the best choice?"

Gennie smiled as if Marrick relayed a joke. "Rule number eighty-seven."

Marrick said nothing, he did not ask what the statement meant. For once he really did not want to know. He remained silent to accept orders.

A single word and the scene would begin. A single word that Gennie would utter, hoped she could utter, prayed would make the commodore proud. "Fire."

"Fire!" Marrick bellowed with more force than Gennie thought possible.

The command ran the length to the gunner at the langshe. The man touched the fuse with the lamp fire in his hand.

Sizzling down the fuse into the first propulsion cavity, the rocket took off into the port and the fully armed array on the beaches.

Gennie watched, unable to contain her glee as the close range into water less dense, moving faster than typical, caused the rocket to propel onto the sandy shore and through several ranks of the sultana's army before the second fuse ignited in the powder-filled tube of the langshe. Bodies, tossed like dolls from the weapon's intensity, flew into the air and sea leaving sprays of bloody geysers in their turning, flipping voyage back to earth.

Gennie wished at that moment to see the look on the commodore's face, or the sultana's for that matter.

"By the gods, that woman is insane." De Xavier watched the scene explode on the Kjoura docks.

He never had the fortune to see *Ecstasy* in action other than the time it was *Despair* in her sights. His galleon lost its adopted sister ship in a storm and for whatever reason *Ecstasy* chose not to return to *Despair*'s side.

He thought of the moments before the battle, on the deck of the junk, standing beside Blackstrap and her eclectic crew who had been gathered from shores near and far, waiting with loyalty in their eyes. De Xavier had not understood how any of the woman's stories were true. He wanted to remember more of the nonsense now, watching fire spew from the monstrous ship, imagining her captain's voice bellowing orders. He wanted to put faces to the names he heard her speak.

Another sparkling langshe burst from the fore of the junk. De Xavier put his spyglass to his eye.

"That was the second," De Xavier called over the ship. "She will send out one more of her dragons before it is our turn. Be certain we are in range."

To himself he thought, looking through the spyglass again, "It will be difficult enough to match that power, but to miss would be an act I will never live down."

"What are they doing!" the sultana screeched. "Why is no one firing upon them?"

The woman swept to the seaside balcony at the highest of

her towers. She put her eye to the scope mounted on the ivory rail.

Her attendees ignored the raging, taking leave to save their own lives instead.

Bint Tariq shadowed the sultana, though there was no rush to her step. In the advisor's eyes, the leader fell the moment the pirate women was allowed back into the harbor alive.

"How did that damned woman escape a second time!" the sultana fumed. "Why is he helping her!"

"You offered so little sultana." Meryem leveled with the woman. "A partnership of that much power is more than you or your kingdom could hope to outweigh."

The sultana turned to glare at the woman. A look that typically would have turned Meryem to cowardice, she took without concern.

"Give the orders to return fire!" the sultana wailed. "Why have the soldiers not been given orders?"

Meryem walked out into the chaos of the castle. She did not tell the sultana that nearly half the cities forces were on the side of the korsana and De Xavier.

The docks exploded into chaos once again as *Despair* took her turn at the target. She may not have the range or unique terrors the junk contained when it came to weapons, but she was in no way short on firepower.

De Xavier ordered all cannons aimed to shore set to fire for the primary assault. They brought from other portions of the ship as many guns as would fit and not cause of the galleon to dip into the sea.

The resulting explosion shuddered the water with such force both *Ecstasy* and *Despair* felt the rumble. It was enough to cause the corresponding collapse of a weakened wall on the cove surrounding the port city. An avalanche of ruble crashed into the waters below.

"Perfect." De Xavier thanked his gods for the added, natural accent to his attack.

"Even without missiles and torpedoes the man still manages to best me," Gennie laughed even as she pouted behind her spyglass.

Not a man of her crew heard the complaint. All cheered with vigor, preparing for their second attack.

Despair and *Ecstasy* closed range on the beach to a distance that even crew without aid of magnifying lenses could see the carnage left by the first volley. The cresting waves were pink with blood as they crashed against broken bodies of the sultana's armies.

Gennie was grateful to see the hazarpatish among her crew. It set Gennie's mind at ease to know she would not have to question his loyalty in the future or fear retribution for any damage she currently caused. She understood it a hard decision for the man, though. The number of years he spent with the sultana's army made the men, whose bodies likely floated in pieces on the beaches, like brothers in some cases. He brought his soldiers with him, but no others dared leave the sultana for fear of death.

"So much for avoiding that," Gennie laughed as another langshe sizzled to life and shot from *Ecstasy*.

A roar like a tidal wave rose from the crew as they watched the weapon, never fired at such a close range to land, skip like flat stone over blood stained waves. In a final leap, aided by a rolling crest, the missile flew over several feet of beach and into buildings closest to shore used for storing small vessels and supplies.

In a burst of sparks and color the building exploded around the glittering langshe.

"AdeebA Korsana!" the sultana raged and beat her fists on the rail. "Fire upon them! Send her and that wretched dingy to the bottom of the harbor!"

De Xavier laughed over the sound of the second firing of

over one hundred cannons on board *Despair*.

The nines fell like a storm of iron hail from the hands of an unnamed angry god of war onto shore, riddling the beach with deep holes and taking many more soldiers to instant burial.

Gennie could contain her emotions no longer. She hopped giddily as she held the rail.

"Six more is all we have left captain!" The gunner's voice boomed through the din.

Gennie turned from the sights on the beach. Her eyes lit like fuses of a langshe. "Fire 'em all! We will shake that chien from her tower. Let's show Kjoura what fireworks are."

The long pause from *Ecstasy*'s attacks caused De Xavier to turn his glass to her decks. They were close enough to feel every shudder from one another and share screams of exhilaration. Gennie, wanting to be certain the commodore watched this, finally locked her glass on De Xavier as he focused on her.

Gennie waved. De Xavier smiled and waved in return.

"Load them all again, and light 'em up," De Xavier commanded. "This is going to be one hell of a finale and I will not be outdone by Cinta."

Through barely tempered rage, M'nef Sheilk, Sultana of Kjoura pulled her eye to the mounted gold and ivory spyglass to look again at the devastation her army and fleet had be come at the hands of two captains.

She focused. The finale struck the sky on fire. One hundred flaming cannon balls, tiny comets hailing apocalypse directly behind fired from both *Ecstasy* and *Despair*. Fires lined the length of beach creating a landing line for the final six langshe, fired, in rapid succession that pushed even the massive *Ecstasy* back from the force, again the sky streaked as hundreds of smaller airborne langshe raced to their prey.

The resulting explosion took another wall from the cove and filled the space from beach to cloud line with sparkling bursts of color. Blood coated the beach, a sticky crimson second ocean. With final shudder that rumbled up the land to the palace, the sultana held the rail of the balcony as she watched the crack spider web up the outer wall of her evacuated castle.

Chapter 33

"So," Gennie sat across from De Xavier in the single-sailed dinghy, "what do we do for an encore?"

De Xavier took a swig from a flask of rum. He passed it to Gennie. "A very good question, but whatever it is, we should work together."

Gennie turned her gaze to the red-gold sky and sun setting on the horizon. *Despair* and *Ecstasy* floated, anchored, side by side.

"They are an interesting pair," she noted and raised the flask to the ships before taking a second swig.

"So are we." De Xavier snagged the flask back from the woman and leaned back against the mast of the dinghy, feet on the wall of the modest vessel.

"C'est vrai." Gennie stretched her small body full length on the bench. "Mais, je suis plus interesant, mon frère." She folded her arms behind her head, and tipped her hat over her face, ignoring the smirk on De Xavier's lips.

More books from Clayborn Press

More Fiction books by other authors:
The Undine Heart
R. L. Spidell
(Available now!)

The Allure of the Mask
R. L. Spidell
(Available Now!)

Words Apart
D. H. Kay
(Available Now!)

Hush, Little Baby
Kaydee Thompson
(Available December, 2010)

More Non-Fiction books by other authors:
Clayborn's Beginner's Guide to Apartments
Johnathan Clayborn
(Available December, 2010)

Clayborn's Beginner's Guide to Motorcycles
Johnathan Clayborn
(Available Now!)

For current information please visit:

www.claybornpress.com

About the Author

J. J. M. Czep

J. J. M. Czep enjoys writing, reading, and teaching creative writing classes. When she is not enjoying literary hobbies she enjoy costume making and belly dancing. She currently lives in Arizona with her husband and her son.